Rebellion

(The Rome's Revolution Saga: Book 2 of 3)

BY
MICHAEL BRACHMAN

REBELLION
(THE ROME'S REVOLUTION SAGA: BOOK 2)

V1.22.0001

Also by Michael Brachman

The Rome's Revolution Series
Rome's Revolution
The Ark Lords
Rome's Evolution

The Rome's Revolution Saga
Rebirth: The Rome's Revolution Saga – Book 1
Rebellion: The Rome's Revolution Saga – Book 2
Redemption: The Rome's Revolution Saga – Book 3

The Vuduri Knights Series
The Milk Run

The Vuduri Universe Series
The Vuduri Companion
Tales of the Vuduri: Year One
Tales of the Vuduri: Year Two
Tales of the Vuduri: Year Three
Tales of the Vuduri: Year Four
Tales of the Vuduri: Year Five

Dedication

Each time I publish a new book, my dedications grow larger because the number of people helping me continues to grow. Even so, first, as always, I must thank my brother Bruce. He has always had my back even before I restarted my modern career. Not only is he my editor and artist and the inspiration behind MINIMCOM, but he is also fiercely protective of the Vuduri culture and characters. Bruce creates the amazing covers, the book trailers and makes my writing so much better. Bruce, I could not have done it without you.

My friend Helen has always been a fantastic sounding board. She is quite a spectacular writer and her advice has always been amazing. For this particular book, she taught me about scene and structure and that help me reorganize the chapters into becoming page turners so you would not be able to ever put the book down. Thank you, Helen, for all your support over the years.

I would like to thank Barbara for always encouraging me, reading these books time and time again and helping me to bring humanity to characters that always teetered on the brink of being two-dimensional. Barbara forced me to consider giving all the characters, even the minor ones, some much needed depth so you would care about them as people.

I would like to thank my countless readers for their criticism and suggestions. Sometimes it stung a little but it was always for a good cause.

Finally, my undying gratitude to my wife, Denise, for all her love and support throughout the entire process. She patiently waits while I hide myself in the basement, cranking out what is now over a million words, because she knows I love writing. She even cooperates and allows me to keep my workspace unadorned, despite the fact that it is against her nature, so that my mind can travel to different places and times. Denise, thank you so much and I'll be up around 5:30, I promise. Yeah, right, she says.

Preface

This story is true. It just hasn't happened yet.

Prologue

Year 3456 AD (1376 PR)
Kuiper Belt, Just Outside the Tau Ceti System
(11.9 Light Years from Earth)

REI BIERAK WAS SOUND ASLEEP IN THE BEDROOM HE SHARED WITH Rome when a slight hiss emitted from the communication grille mounted directly above the headboard. It was 11 months into their year-long journey from Tabit to Deucado, during the interval designated as nighttime even though here in the blackness of space such a distinction was completely arbitrary. Their bedroom was nestled inside the converted Vuduri space tug affectionately known as the Flying House.

`"Psst, Rei,"` MINIMCOM whispered from the grille however he received no response.

After waiting a moment, the little computer spoke again, this time a bit louder, `"Please wake up, Rei."`

Eyes still closed, Rei asked in a fatigued tone, "What is it, MINIMCOM?"

`"I need you to look at something."`

The 26-year-old man from the 21st century opened his eyes. He turned to his left and saw that Rome was still fast asleep.

"Hold on," he said wearily. He jumped up and padded into the refresher, closing the door behind him. Standing at the sink, he splashed some water onto his face and peered into his reflection.

"Vroggon Chrosd ta Jasus," Rei said out loud, shaking his head.

`"You speak Vuduri even when alone?"` MINIMCOM asked from a grille mounted to the left of the sink.

"That's all we use now. You know that. I have to keep practicing. Rome says nobody is going to take the time to learn English on Deucado. Especially the mandasurte. And she's right."

`"Very well. Fiu veler ebanes am Vuduri."`

"I don't need help from you," Rei said sharply. He paused for a moment. "Sorry. I didn't mean to snap at you, I'm just tired."

`"No need to apologize. As I have stated on numerous occasions, I do not have feelings."`

"Well, I do," Rei said, "and I'm really worried about Rome. She's barely halfway through the third trimester but the baby's getting so big. She has trouble breathing all the time."

"We will be arriving at Deucado within three weeks. There you will have access to medical aid. My readings tell me she will be able to make it until then."

"Yeah, I know," Rei said, straightening up. "Forget I said anything. So tell me, what's so important that you had to wake me up in the middle of the night?"

"We are about to enter the Kuiper Belt surrounding the star system. The Belt contains an unusually large amount of mass - comets, asteroids and the like. I have been using the starprobes in a dense array to chart a safe way through and they found something."

"What kind of something?"

"An anomalous object, far too regularly shaped to be natural."

"Are you saying it's man-made?"

"That would be presumptuous. I would prefer that we use the term artificial for the time being."

"Regardless, what do you think it is?"

"I do not know. That is why I need you to look at it and determine if it is important."

"OK," Rei said, yawning. He opened the door to the refresher and saw Rome standing there, looking as pregnant as humanly possible.

"Qua asde onti sipra?" Rome asked, rubbing her eyes.

"MINIMCOM's found something that he needs me to look at," Rei answered. "It's probably nothing but I told him I'd go up to the cockpit and see."

"I will go with you." Rome turned toward the entrance to the bedroom then cried out in pain.

"What is it, honey?" Rei asked, rushing over to her. "Your breath?"

"No," Rome said, reaching behind her with her arm. "It is my back. It has been hurting more and more."

Rei stared at her for a second then snapped his fingers. "Stay right here," he said. He dashed out of the room and returned a moment later with a large white bottle and a squeeze bulb of water.

"Hold this for a sec," he said, handing her the squeeze bulb. He opened the bottle and shook out one pill.

"Are those not the pills for your people when we land on Deucado?" Rome asked.

"Yeah," Rei said, staring at the pill. "My back was killing me when I was first awakened. OMCOM made these to compensate for 1400 years worth of degeneration. I'm betting they'll do wonders for you. We have plenty to spare."

"But my back is Vuduri, do you think these pills will even work?" Rome paused for a moment. "And more importantly, do you think they might affect the baby? I cannot ingest anything that could be harmful."

"Good point," Rei said. He looked back to the grille mounted over the sink. "Hey MINIMCOM...those pills that OMCOM gave me. Will they help Rome's back? Is there any chance they'll hurt her or the baby?"

"They will have absolutely no negative effect on the baby. As to whether they will help Rome's back, I cannot be sure. On balance, I would say yes. Either way, I cannot compute a downside to trying."

Rei started to hand the pill to Rome then drew his hand back.

"What is it?" Rome asked.

"I don't know," Rei answered, looking puzzled. "I thought the pill that OMCOM gave me was yellow. This one is white."

"Do you think it makes a difference?"

"No clue," Rei replied reflectively. He held the bottle up to his eye and jostled it around, peering into it. He spotted one yellow pill mixed among all the other white ones. He shook out a bunch and picked out the yellow one and handed it to Rome.

"No sense in mixing apples and oranges," he said.

"What has fruit got to do with this?" Rome asked with a bewildered look on her face.

"It's just an expression," Rei replied, laughing gently.

"How long until the pill takes effect?"

"When I took mine, I was a lot better in just a few days," he answered. "OMCOM said in my case, it would take almost a full year for the effects to become complete. Right now, I'd say my back is mostly perfect. But for you, I'm guessing it'll help within a day or so."

"Good," Rome said, swallowing the pill. "I could use the relief." She smiled and pointed to the door. "You go on up to the cockpit. I will meet you up there in a minute."

"Sure," Rei bent over and gave Rome a kiss. "See you shortly." He left the bedroom and headed forward.

It was longer than one minute but eventually, Rome entered the cockpit and sat down in the co-pilot's seat.

"What have you found?" she asked, breathing heavily.

"I'm not sure," Rei answered, pointing at the viewscreen. "MINIMCOM detected something odd floating in space. We're trying to figure out what it is. The starprobes weren't built for close up inspection. But MINIMCOM is right. It certainly isn't natural."

Rome observed the image on the center viewscreen. There were quite a few objects, mostly boulder-shaped, spinning very slowly. On the right viewscreen, MINIMCOM had reconstructed a still snapshot of the object in question. The image was blurry but Rome could see it was elongated, rectangular and its edges were distinctly regular.

"MINIMCOM, how far away is the object?" she asked.

"Only a few light minutes."

"What do you think, Rome?" Rei asked. "MINIMCOM says he can get us there in a single jump. Should we go take a look?"

"Yes. Since it is not really out of our way, it is worthy of inspection."

"OK, MINIMCOM. Go ahead and plot the jump," Rei commanded.

"I have already performed the necessary calculations."

"Great," Rei responded. "In that case, you can fire when ready, Gridley."

"My name is MINIMCOM. Why are you calling me Gridley?"

"Never mind," Rei said, chuckling. "Just go ahead."

MINIMCOM activated the PPT generators and their high-pitched whine. Having heard the sound thousands of times over the last 11 months, Rome and Rei had long since stopped paying it any attention. But for this excursion, the sound was quite noticeable. In front of them, the dark circle of negative energy grew larger and larger, exposing the stars on the far side. Their destination star, Tau Ceti, shined a tiny bit brighter than before. When the tunnel reached maximum size, MINIMCOM fired the plasma thrusters on both tugs and the combined mass of the two ships plus Rei's Ark inched into the hole. As soon as they were completely though, they heard the regular thunk-clunk of MINIMCOM disengaging and reengaging such that he could use his plasma thrusters to bring them to a halt.

"Did you do it?" Rei asked.

"Yes. The object is to your left approximately one hundred and fifty thousand kilometers."

The central section of the large flat-panel monitor built into the front console lit up but it only showed the cold, clear darkness of interplanetary space.

"Where is it, MINIMCOM?" Rome asked. "I do not see anything." She squinted flipping between regular vision and her telescopic vision but nothing resolved itself.

A set of sequentially widening circles appeared on the center of the screen, reminiscent of a radar sweep or an air traffic controller's screen. If the purpose of the circles was to locate the object, there was nothing there.

"I don't see anything either. Can you switch to infrared?" Rei asked.

"The object is sitting at ambient. That would not make it any more visible."

"So how can you detect it?" Rei asked.

"MIDAR."

"So show us the MIDAR screen," Rei said exhaustedly.

The screen switched to a set of fixed concentric circles and within the circles, a bright line appeared as it swept clockwise. When the sweeping hand hit the 11 o'clock position, a tiny dot flashed. As MIDAR was three-dimensional, it was easy to see that the object lay below the plane of their current trajectory.

"Can you magnify it?"

"Of course," replied MINIMCOM. The concentric circles slid off the screen zooming into just segments of arc. The object they were tracking became centered. MINIMCOM suppressed the reflections of the extraneous mass surrounding the object but there was no legend to gauge its overall size.

"What are its dimensions?" Rei asked.

"The object is approximately two meters long by one and a half meters tall by one meter deep."

"Omigod," Rei exclaimed.

"What?" Rome asked. "What do you think it is?"

"You're not going to believe this," Rei answered. "But I think it's a sarcophagus. That's the exact right dimensions."

"What is it doing out here?"

Rei shook his head. "Our ship was headed toward this star system. Based upon how messed up the Ark is, I think we hit something along the way in. I'm assuming the collision sheared off the command compartment. This must be one of the command crew."

Rome looked at image again then turned toward Rei. "What do you want to do?"

He cocked his head. "We have to go get it, of course."

"In our current configuration that would not be very practical. It would be far more efficient if I detached from the Ark and flew my tug there."

Rei glanced at the screen then looked up at Rome, questioningly. She was scowling.

"Rome, come on," he said. "It's one of my people. We can't just leave him here in space. I've gotta go and get him. I'd take you with me but in your condition…" Rei pointed to her protruding belly.

"But, but," Rome stammered.

"What is it, honey?" Rei asked tenderly.

"What if something happens to you? I will not be able to help you." A tear came to her eye. "I would just die if anything happened to you."

"Nothing's going to happen," Rei replied, reaching forward to wipe away the tear. "I'll be careful, I promise." He turned toward the viewscreen. "MINIMCOM, I need about five minutes to get ready."

"How will you get here?"

"I won't. You come get me."

"Of course," MINIMCOM responded. **"I will be there momentarily."** The little computer's words were punctuated with a clunk as the tug disengaged the magnetic clamps.

Rei hopped up to aid Rome out of her seat. They made their way to the side airlock, where Rome helped Rei get into his pressure suit. He pulled the hand thruster down from the shelf and clipped it to his belt. Looking down, he saw the case containing the VIRUS units and picked it up and secured the case to his belt as well.

"Why are you taking that?" Rome asked.

"It always gave me the willies to keep those things here," he said. "I'm going to take them over and leave them aboard MINIMCOM. I just never had a chance before."

"I understand. I think that is a good idea as well."

Rei picked up his helmet. He leaned forward and puckered his lips. Rome kissed him but there was no ardor. The kiss was perfunctory.

"What?" he asked, peering into Rome's eyes which were glowing with the light reflecting off of her tapetum. Tears were streaming down both cheeks now.

"Rei," she answered finally. "I am afraid. You will be leaving me alone."

"It'll be fine," Rei said, trying to be upbeat. "This isn't the first time we've done this. Remember when I went out to jettison the propulsion unit?"

"Yes, but that time you were tethered to this tug during the entire mission. And I was able to see you. You did not really go anywhere. This time, you and MINIMCOM are going to fly away from here. This is the first time in my life that I will ever be truly alone."

"It's not like Cesdiud. I'll have MINIMCOM hook up a video and audio link. We'll talk the whole time. It'll be like I'm right there with you."

Rome sighed. "It will not be the same but I suppose I must learn to do it at some point. You go. I will be all right."

Rei leaned forward and kissed her again lightly. This time, Rome grabbed his head with both hands and kissed him long and passionately, making the man dizzy.

"You be careful, Rei Bierak. You come back to me," Rome said firmly.

"Nothing will ever keep us apart," Rei vowed earnestly. "I promise."

Looking sad, Rome stepped back out of the airlock. Rei engaged his helmet. The door closed and Rome leaned forward to peer at him through the porthole. He turned to look at her and had a sudden feeling of déjà vu. Rome put her hand up to the glass and Rei placed his gloved hand against hers. She nodded.

With that, Rei turned and pressed the stud to activate the outer door. He could feel his suit stiffen as pumps worked to pull the air out of the airlock, leaving the chamber in a near vacuum. The differential indicator turned red and the outer door opened automatically.

Not even six feet away, MINIMCOM's tug hovered in place with the side airlock directly across from Rei. The outer door was already open. Rei looked back at Rome one more time then took a flying leap and landed inside the other tug with nary a jolt. Rei closed the outer airlock door then quickly made his way to the archway that served as the secondary airlock and entry to the cockpit, closing the door behind him. As soon as the indicator turned green, the door opened and Rei stepped through.

He surveyed the cockpit. Its layout was identical to his own tug's cockpit, with the exception of a large white box bolted on the floor where the co-pilot's seat had been. Rei set the carrying case holding the VIRUS units on the floor and removed his helmet. The air smelled musty. There had been nothing here to stir it up in almost a year.

"MINIMCOM?" he said, bending forward and tapping the rectangular box.

"Pleased to make your acquaintance," came a tinny voice from the grille mounted on the front instrument panel.

"This is weird, huh? We've spent the last year together but I've never actually seen you before."

"Impressive, am I not?" MINIMCOM said regally.

Rei laughed. "Yes, you are," he said. "Before we do anything, can you patch me through to Rome? I think she was about to have a conniption."

"What is a conniption?"

"You don't want to know," Rei replied. "Just patch me through. Please."

"Connecting."

"Romey?" Rei asked tentatively.

Her beautiful image appeared on the viewscreen. "Yes, mau emir. I am here."

"Well, you can see that I made it OK, right?"

"Yes," Rome replied tersely.

"So you can relax now, right, honey?" Rei asked.

"That is too much to ask but I am happy that you are safe."

"OK. Sweetheart, we're going to head out now."

"I will be here, monitoring."

"Okeydokey," Rei replied. He pointed to the case on the floor. "I brought you a present, MINIMCOM."

"The VIRUS units. You are too kind. If it would not be too much trouble, would you mind securing them in one of the storage compartments? I would rather they not rattle around while I perform my maneuvers."

A bin popped open on the far side of the cabin.

"No problem," Rei said, shaking his head. After securing the case, he closed the cabinet door and then made his to the pilot's seat on the left. He buckled himself into the long-vacant chair, checking the X-harness for snugness.

"OK. I'm ready. What say we go and retrieve my comrade?"

"Very well, sir," MINIMCOM replied obediently. Rei stifled a chuckle.

MINIMCOM fired short bursts on the trim-jets until it cleared the Ark by about 50 meters then the little computer ignited the plasma thrusters. Quickly their velocity climbed to 150 km/sec. MINIMCOM shut down the engines and they coasted. It only took them about 15 minutes to traverse the 150,000 kilometers to the object. As they approached, MINIMCOM fired the trim-jets to decelerate, coming to a dead halt no more than 100 meters from the sarcophagus nestled among a group of fairly large boulders. Rei flipped on the powerful front floodlights and illuminated their quarry. Now that it was visible, Rei could see that the sarcophagus was a dull gray but had three broad red stripes around it.

"It's Captain Keller," Rei announced.

"How can you tell?" Rome asked.

"They put red stripes around the chambers for the command crew. Three stripes means Captain."

Rei looked down at the MIDAR display and then back up at the sarcophagus.

"OK, MINIMCOM, turn around and back in as close as you dare. I'm going to go out and…"

"Rei!" Rome shouted.

"Don't worry, sweetheart," Rei said. "I'll be tethered in the whole time. The hand thruster is all I need."

"Be very careful," Rome admonished. "You know there are no radios in our pressure suits. If you run into any problems, tug twice on the tether. MINIMCOM, you will watch him and at the first sign of trouble, you get him out of there."

"**Affirmative.**"

The retrieval operation went fairly smoothly. Rei had a little trouble grabbing onto the railing surrounding the sarcophagus but once he gripped it, he was able to swing up and straddle it like a would-be cowboy on an artificial bull. A few short bursts of the hand thruster extricated the sarcophagus from its rocky neighbors. A couple more bursts and Rei and his ride glided smoothly back to the waiting confines of MINIMCOM's cargo compartment. The cargo ramp and hatch closed to form a tight seal and MINIMCOM repressurized the compartment.

Rei disengaged and floated away from the coffin-like object. Once he was clear, ever so slowly, MINIMCOM re-activated the artificial gravity. The heavy object settled gently onto the cargo bay floor. At this point, Rei removed his helmet and walked over to the sarcophagus.

While the faceplate was completely iced over, the nameplate said "Captain M. Keller" confirming Rei's suspicions. He inspected every inch of the top of the sarcophagus, looking for cracks. He found none.

"I can't believe it but it looks intact. He may still be alive."

Rei stooped down, examining the rods and panel, locating the handles he needed to turn to begin the thaw cycle.

"Wait," Rome's voice rang out from a grille mounted in the cargo bay.

"What?" Rei said.

"What are you doing?"

"I was going to reanimate him, of course," Rei said, confused.

"I do not think you should do that."

Rei stood up and looked over at the wall.

"Why?" Rei asked. "I need to awaken him."

"Think about it," Rome explained. "When we first reanimated you at Skyler Base, you were weak and disoriented. If your Captain requires any kind of medical attention, we are not equipped to provide it."

"But, but…" Rei said. "We should…"

"Rei," she said sternly. "There is no food or water there. You have no way to get him over here. Remember, we will be arriving at Deucado in three weeks. Why not just wait until then to thaw him out?"

"But the temperature in here, it might trigger the thaw cycle automatically," Rei protested.

"I will keep the cargo bay evacuated and the temperature will be very close to space ambient."

Rei was silent for a moment as he thought about their words. After a few seconds, he nodded. "You're right. If he's still alive after 1300 years of being frozen and floating around in space, another three weeks isn't going to kill him. MINIMCOM, can you tell if there are any other crew members in the area?"

"I have searched extensively with MIDAR and the starprobes. I have found none."

"Oh," Rei said, a bit crestfallen.

"If it is any consolation, I will leave a beacon here in case any ships have the opportunity to search the area again."

"OK," Rei said. "I guess that's the best we can do."

After securing the sarcophagus with some short tethers stored in the cargo bay, Rei spoke up. "All right, MINIMCOM, he'll be safe here by himself. I'm ready to get back to Rome."

"Affirmative," replied MINIMCOM.

"Thank you," came Rome's voice. "I miss you too much already."

Chapter 1

(Three weeks later)
Second Planet (Deucado), Tau Ceti System
(11.9 Light Years from Earth)

REI LOOKED OVER AT ROME, WHO WAS FIDGETING AROUND UNCOMfortably in the co-pilot's chair.

"Final jump," he mused. "Excited?"

"Yes, of course," she replied. She considered her own words. "Perhaps relieved is more like it." She pointed to her abdomen. It looked like she had swallowed a watermelon. "But in some ways, I will miss this tug."

"Miss it? Why? Haven't we been stuck here long enough?"

Rome looked at him. "Yes, but it does not feel like being stuck. Not with you. This was our first home together. It will always be special to me."

"Yeah, to me too, I guess," Rei said, sighing. He glanced back briefly at the airlock.

Rome reached behind and pulled the two straps downwards. She struggled to attach the X-harness, having to arrange it so it didn't press on her belly.

While she was fiddling, Rei spoke again. "I am so looking forward to this. Plus I miss real gravity. Do you want to know the first thing I'm going to do when we land?"

"Exit the tug?" Rome said with a straight face.

Rei laughed. "I meant after that."

"I knew what you meant," Rome said, breaking out into a smile.

"Ha. I'm going to take a long walk with you," Rei offered.

"Why?" Rome asked.

"Just because we can."

"Yes but I suspect I will not want to walk as far as you."

"Yeah, right." Rei looked down at the grille mounted in the console. "Hey MINIMCOM, what's the plan, buddy?" Rei asked.

"Less than five minutes to jump. I want to get us as close to the planet as possible so I am using several autonomous algorithms to calculate the jump for cross-correlation. Buddy."

"OK," Rei said, laughing. He leaned back in his seat even though there was not much play in the high-g harness. "Romey, where should we try and land?"

"We will let the authorities on Deucado decide that," she answered.

"Sure, that makes sense. We've always assumed my people are going to want to go off and live by themselves. Maybe they don't have to. I think maybe the mixing of the two cultures would be a good thing. Your people can certainly teach mine a thing or two and I'm sure there is some technology that isn't forbidden or at least a point of view that we can contribute."

"I agree," Rome replied. "However, this will have to be up to the parties involved. You and I will just have to wait until we get there to see how things play out."

"Agreed."

"Calculations complete," MINIMCOM announced. **"One minute to jump."**

"Great," Rei exclaimed. He rubbed his hands together. Then he looked over at Rome's stomach again.

"Honey, for landing, we're going to have to squeeze you into a pressure suit, just in case, right?"

Rome wagged a finger at him. "I will manage," she said tersely.

He continued. "Well, we have a spare suit. I was thinking we could stitch the two together…"

"Whatever you are about to say," Rome interrupted, "do not dare!" Her glowing eyes were flashing but there was a smile on her face.

Rei laughed. "I understand."

"Initiating jump," MINIMCOM announced.

The PPT generators attached to the airfoils ramped up. The high-pitched whine coincided with a bright circle that appeared well in front of the ship. At its center was a tiny blue jewel. Rei could barely sit still. That was Deucado dead ahead.

As soon as the circle was complete, the plasma thrusters fired, pushing Rei and Rome gently back into their seats. The whole construct moved forward and, in a flash, they were through. The star called Tau Ceti was now off to their left and slightly behind the windshield. For the moment, the tiny blue jewel in front of them was the brightest object in the sky.

"Look at that!" Rei exclaimed. "That is awesome!"

"Yes," Rome replied. "Beautiful, is it not?"

"Sure is," Rei answered admiringly.

"Please look to your right."

"Where?" he asked.

"As you would say, the two o'clock position."

Rei looked and saw nothing spectacular. Rome pointed and said, "There, that star?" she asked. "Is that what you are referring to?"

"That is not a star. That is a gas giant, roughly four times the size of Jupiter. Grentadar is the third planet out in this system."

"OK," said Rei. "So what?"

"From its proximity to Deucado, it is likely that it has deflected or absorbed much of the extraneous mass that has entered the inner perimeter. Based upon how much matter we observed in the Kuiper Belt, I would have estimated that Deucado would be subject to a higher-than-expected amount of bombardment of comets, meteors and asteroids."

Rei replied. "What has one got to do with the other?"

"Based upon the proximity between the two planets, it may explain why life was able to develop on Deucado. Perhaps Grentadar acted like a shield."

"That seems logical," Rome said.

"Whatever," Rei interjected. "I've got a better idea. Why don't we go to Deucado and find out?"

"Very well," replied MINIMCOM in a fussy tone and with that, he ignited the plasma engines full bore. Rome and Rei were pushed gently back into their seats once again, as the tugs and the Ark began to accelerate. MINIMCOM displayed the flight path required to put the Ark into high orbit around Deucado. Once he was satisfied with their speed, MINIMCOM cut out the thrusters and they coasted toward the planet.

Rei looked at Rome, his beautiful Rome, sitting there, as pregnant as a person could be without bursting. He loved her more than life itself. He watched her grimace slightly.

"Kicking again?"

"Yes," she replied. Rome looked down at her abdomen and pointed to it. "It is a boy, you know."

"A boy!" Rei exclaimed. "I'm going to have a son? Oh Rome," he sighed. "What did I ever do to deserve you?"

"I do not know but I must have done the same thing. We were just meant to be together. Forever."

"Forever's good enough for me. How's about we get you into that pressure suit?"

"All right," Rome said and with some struggling, the two of them addressed that issue.

After Rei and Rome were finished getting dressed, they came forward and strapped themselves in again.

"We are coming up on the day-night terminator. You can see some planetary features if you examine the relief caused by the shadows."

They could see the dividing line between daylight and nighttime sweeping across the western side of the planet. As they got closer still, two tiny bright dots appeared, one on each side of the planet.

"Those must be the two natural satellites of Deucado, Mockay and Givy," Rome said.

"Which one is which?"

"Mockay is smaller and closer to the planet. I believe it is that one," she replied, pointing to the moon on the left. "The other is Givy. It is much larger but also much farther away. From the ground, I would expect they appear nearly the same size."

"I guess we'll see when we get there," Rei observed.

"Which will be very soon," MINIMCOM interjected.

Rei and Rome both watched with wide-eyed fascination as the blue jewel grew larger and larger. Whereas earlier, it had been marble-sized and then basketball-sized, now it was filling their whole field of view. They quickly passed into the night side.

Within their cabin, Rei and Rome heard the standard thump and delayed clunk as MINIMCOM reversed the orientation of his tug and fired his plasma thrusters, slowing the assembly gradually as they swung past the planet.

At last, MINIMCOM announced, **"Orbit achieved."**

Rei looked at Rome. "Honey, we're home," he said with a broad smile on his face.

Rome nodded and watched intently as they were coming up on the dawn side. Where the sun was illuminating the water, the deep blue oceans sparkled crisply from their high angle. Although there were large sections covered by heavy white clouds, much of the planet's surface was easily viewed. This planet had roughly an equal distribution of land and water. The majority of the land mass was contained within two major continents, with the one divided nearly in half with a relatively narrow isthmus connecting the northern and southern halves. As they moved around past the ocean and over the land, they could see the one continent had a Swiss cheese-like appearance. All across the surface there were many, many lakes and inland seas, most of them circular or rounded.

"Look at all the holes," Rei said.

"Yes. Despite what MINIMCOM said about a shield, they must be due to a substantial number of collisions with comets and such," Rome observed.

"Most of them seem soft, not sharp like you see on the moon. Have there been any reports of bombardment since the Vuduri have been here?"

"Not that I am aware of."

"Well, it looks good to me. There and there," Rei pointed down, "there's a ton of bright yellow and green coloration. That has to be vegetation."

"Oh yes, there is much vegetation," Rome replied.

Without warning, the central display lit up and in front of them sat a gray-haired Vuduri man.

"Who are you?" he asked in Vuduri. "We do not detect any PPT resonance."

"We are mandasurte," Rome answered. "We have come from the Tabit stellar observatory. We are towing one of the ancient Essessoni Arks that we found there."

The man's eyes grew wide then narrowed. In a flat voice, he said, "On this world, mandasurte in possession of Vuduri technology is a capital crime. You have condemned yourself. You will die."

The screen went black.

"What the hell!?" Rei shouted.

The MIDAR display lit up.

"The Vuduri have just launched multiple craft. They appear to be armed."

"Vuduri do not use weapons," Rome insisted.

"These do."

"Forget that. What do we do? MINIMCOM, can we outrun them?" Rei asked, his voice rising.

"Not with your cargo craft."

"And if we left it here?"

"Rome already told them it was an Ark. They will assume the Erklirte have returned."

"Can you get them back on the comm? Their rules should not apply to us. We are supposed to be here." Rome asked, desperately.

"I have already tried. There is no reply. You should determine a course of action and quickly. I believe you should take evasive maneuvers immediately!"

"What kind of arms are they carrying?" Rei asked anxiously.

"Magnetic pulse cannons, electrostatic charge disrupters and PPT throwers."

Rome gasped. All the color left her face.

"What? Say again," Rei asked.

"PPT throwers."

"What are those?" he asked, panicked.

"They are normally used in mining and salvage operations on the surface. They create a moving PPT tunnel. They can cut through any material known to man. However, in space, they can extend over a much greater distance."

"So you're saying…" Rei sputtered.

"What he is saying," Rome barked, "is that they are for slicing up very large objects into very tiny pieces."

"How much time do we have?" Rei asked grimly.

"I would estimate ten minutes or less."

Rei looked down at Deucado. After nearly a year, they were so close and now they were never going to see their new home. He looked up at the top of the cabin as if there was somewhere else to go. Suddenly, it came to him.

"I've got it," he said. He tried to snap his fingers but the gloves from the pressure suit prevented it from sounding effective.

"What?" Rome asked.

"We go to the planet."

"We cannot do that, Rei. We are using the EG lifters to hold onto your Ark. We would not survive reentry without the lifters. We would burn up."

"No, no, no. Let me explain." Rei said. "MINIMCOM, what would happen if we open up a PPT tunnel to the surface of the planet?"

"You cannot form a large enough PPT tunnel on the surface of a planet," Rome protested. "There is too much gravitational stress. The tunnel would collapse immediately."

"Rei is correct. For such a short distance, 160 kilometers, the tunnel would actually be stable for sufficient time. However, once the tunnel was formed, the atmosphere of the planet would begin venting out. We would face a formidable wind."

"Nothing that the plasma thrusters couldn't push against, right?" Rei asked.

"Agreed. We would be able to enter the tunnel. But when we emerge, you must still consider Rome's original point. Once we passed through the tunnel, the tugs would have no lift since the EG pods are currently used to secure your crew compartment. We would fall to the surface."

"So we let the Ark go. Once it starts through the tunnel, wouldn't gravity pull the rest through?"

"What purpose would it serve to take the Ark through, just to let it fall to earth and be destroyed?" Rome asked.

"Not if we work it just right…MINIMCOM, can you make the tunnel open up exactly the length of the Ark above the surface?"

MINIMCOM did not answer right away. Finally, he said, **"Yes."**

"OK. Romey, do they have trees down there?"

"Yes. They have cane-tree forests covering most of both continents."

"So that's where we set down. MINIMCOM opens the tunnel up exactly the height of the ship. The Ark goes through the tunnel and touches the ground. Once it's through, we just let it topple over. The trees will break its fall. Everything is secured against stresses way higher than that, including the people. The front part was designed to hit even at terminal velocity. It'll be OK."

"What about us?" Rome asked.

"As soon as the Ark starts through and gravity takes over, we let go and use the EG lifters. We just squirt through when we have enough lift to land. That is if we have enough time to spin up the superconductors,"

"It will be close but my calculations confirm the interval be sufficient."

"OK. What am I missing?" Rei asked. "MINIMCOM, what about our orbital velocity, relative to the ground?"

"I will aim the tunnel tangential to our current orbit. I will make the distance equal to our rate of travel which will negate our velocity. As the ship passes through the tunnel, on the other side, the net velocity relative to the ground will be zero. However such a tunnel will most likely shear off the wings of your Ark."

"Screw it," Rei said. "We don't need them."

"MINIMCOM, can this really work?" Rome inquired.

"I will run a quick simulation and calculate the probability of success."

"I am certain that this has never been tried before."

"But does that mean it won't work," Rei stated fervently. "Right, MINIMCOM?"

"I have completed my calculations. With certain precautions, it has a fairly reasonable probability of success. But I would be remiss if I did not state that it is highly inadvisable."

"What's our alternative?" asked Rei. "Sit here and die? Let them kill us? Kill my people?"

"You have a valid point. If we are to attempt this, we should start as soon as possible. The Vuduri are less than five minutes away from intercept."

"Romey, are you OK with this?" Rei asked.

"Yes, mau emir. I trust you," she said sadly. "And, as you said, what choice do we have?"

"OK, MINIMCOM, take over," Rei insisted.

"Turn the PPT rings for minimum diameter," MINIMCOM said. "I will initiate. Where do you want to set down?"

"Aim for Asquarti, the Western continent," Rome replied, trying to stay calm. "That is where the mandasurte live."

"OK, MINIMCOM, put us down there," Rei ordered.

"Rei, they will come looking for us as soon as they realize what has happened," Rome said worriedly.

"We'll have to figure out something when we get there. We'll hide the ship under some leaves or something. OK?" Rei looked at her. "Are you ready, Romey? You have to fly. I'm not ready for this," he asked less than authoritatively.

Rome closed her eyes. She frowned. She slapped her temple three times, as if trying to jar something loose.

"What's the matter?" Rei asked.

"My bloco and stilo. They have stopped working," Rome replied.

"Can you fly without them?"

"Of course," Rome said. "They just make it easier." She held her arm and hand out to where Rei could get to it. Rei reached out to take it. Even though they were wearing gloves, they gripped each other's hand tightly.

"I am ready," Rome said, "go ahead, MINIMCOM. Execute."

"Calculating jump," MINIMCOM said, then, **"Coordinates ready."**

"Do it!" Rei commanded.

The trim-jets on both tugs fired and rotated the assembled craft so that their tug's nose was pointing directly toward the planet. Rei let go of Rome's hand and grabbed a hold of his armrests. Pointing straight at the surface like this was giving him a bit of vertigo.

"Initiating jump," said MINIMCOM.

Rei and Rome heard the high-pitched whine of their PPT generators revving up. In front of them, a brightly lit hole appeared. Leaves, branches, dirt and dust started shooting out from it. The wind began to buffet the conjoined mass but the trim-jets were sufficient to keep them stable long enough. As the hole widened, they could see the bright yellow-green forest beckoning to them through the onrushing gale. They were looking down, right at it.

MINIMCOM fired the plasma thrusters on their tug, forcing the leading edge of the Ark forward into the tunnel. After a very short time, the little computer shut their thrusters off but they could feel the ship accelerating which meant gravity was taking over.

"Release your clamps," MINIMCOM shouted above the howling which was the wind against their hull. **"The magnets should begin spinning up immediately."**

Rome punched some buttons on the control panel and even though the motion was slight, they began to move off, away from the Ark.

"Your EG lifters are ready. I would suggest manual control from here on in. I will be busy."

"What do you mean? What are you going to do?" Rei asked.

"I must remain attached until the Ark clears the tunnel. I am going to use my plasma thrusters to brake. I cannot let the ship hit the ground too quickly."

"Will you have enough time to break loose?" Rome asked.

"The probability is very low," MINIMCOM said. **"I do not think so."**

"MINIMCOM!" Rei shouted. "What did you do? Why didn't you tell us?"

Quietly, MINIMCOM said, **"I did not trust you to allow me to do what I had to do. This was the only way to save your Ark."**

"You can't…" Rei stopped speaking. Their nose was entering the tunnel and they were looking straight down into the trees. Rocks and branches were banging off them right and left. The powerful wind buffeted their ship and the tinted windshield was starting to ice up.

"What is that? Rome, what's going on? What's happening?"

Rome looked at the instrument panel. "The tug is sitting at minus 80 degrees Celsius, the temperature of space. That must be atmospheric moisture condensing on the ship," she called out.

As soon as their tail was clear of the tunnel, Rome pulled back savagely on both sticks and they could feel the nose beginning to rotate as the trim-jets fired and tug struggled to right itself. The windshield was now covered with frost so thick that they could not make out anything. Rome slammed one throttle forward to force the lead repulsor field to angle their nose higher more quickly; then she pulled back to lift the tug up and away from the rapidly approaching canopy of trees to try to get level. She allowed the joysticks to return to their upright position then she fired the plasma thrusters, jolting them back in their seats. She shut them down a few seconds later. Even though it felt like they were level, Rei's pilot's instincts told him not to trust his senses.

"Can you tell where the Ark is coming down?" Rei shouted. He couldn't see anything through the ice.

"No. I must move off a safe distance then we will come back around when we can see again," Rome replied in a level voice. "Can you activate the MIDAR?"

"Go," he said. He leaned forward to press a few icons as Rome pulled back on both sticks and the tug lurched ahead, gaining altitude. They could hear branches and other debris striking the underside of their craft but they were definitely going up. Soon, the scraping noises subsided and they were in the clear, albeit blindly. Rome studied the displays, trying to get herself oriented. Just then they heard a tremendous crash.

Instinctively, Rei whipped his head around but there was nothing to see except the rear bulkhead of the cockpit. He turned back around and quickly pressed a button to activate one of the rear cameras but all he saw was translucent sheet of ice.

"I can't see anything. Set her down, Romey, set her down," Rei cried out.

"All right," she said, calmly.

Rome peered down at the instruments and toggled the display to MIDAR. She pointed to one section. "There appears to be a small clearing. I will try and set down there."

Rei looked forward and could see nothing but the bright ice. He closed his eyes. This was not what he had planned.

Rome pressed a button on the front display. She stared at it then pressed it again, twice. Frustrated, she banged at it with her fist.

"What?" Rei asked.

"I cannot get the landing gear extended," Rome said worriedly. "The doors will not open. It must be the ice."

"Do we need them? Can you land without them?"

"Yes," Rome replied. "I can do it. I just have to be careful."

It took all of Rome's concentration to bring them to a dead stop, hovering above the clearing, using the MIDAR as a guide. Gently, she lowered the ship, paying careful attention to the altimeter. All along the hull, there were crackling noises but at last, they felt themselves touch down. Rome took her hand off the sticks and sat back in her chair and breathed a huge sigh.

"You did it, Romey." Rei said with relief.

"We did it," Rome corrected him.

"Yes, we…" Rei frowned then opened his eyes wide. "Oh, no," he exclaimed, "MINIMCOM!"

He leaned forward and shouted into the grille mounted on the front panel, "MINIMCOM, are you there?" The only sound they heard was water running somewhere off in the distance.

"MINIMCOM, can you hear us?" Rome said.

Again, there was no answer.

"We've got to go see," Rei said. "Let's go."

Rome nodded and released her high-g harness. She tried to stand up but fell back into the seat immediately. Deucado had a gravity that was 91% of Earth and their long exposure to one-third g, despite all their exercise, left them somewhat ill-prepared. Rei unbuckled himself and stood up, a bit wobbly, but still able to handle it. He stepped over to Rome and bent down.

"Put your arms around my neck," he said.

She reached up for him and pulled him down to her. She kissed him and said, "No matter what happens, mau emir, know that I love you."

"I know you do, honey. I love you, too. We'll be OK. Let me pull you up."

He put his hands on her waist and arched backwards and was pleasantly surprised to see that he had no pain whatsoever. His motion pulled Rome forward and then she was able to stand on her own.

"Are you all right? Can you walk?" Rei asked.

"Yes, I can walk." She steadied herself on the armrest of the chair and moved around it. Rei left her there and made his way over to the inside door of the airlock. He pressed the stud to open it and as soon as he was through, he opened the outer door. Together, hands against the walls, Rome and Rei made their way down the hallway to the far end of the cargo compartment.

Rei pushed the blue stud to raise the cargo door and lower the ramp. Sitting with their belly on the ground, the ramp would not extend very far. As the hatch struggled to open against the coating of ice, it complained by way of some groaning noises but then with a crack, it broke free and the door began to open. The light was so bright that Rei had to hold his arm up to shield his eyes. With Rome's advanced optics, she had no such problem.

Rei just shut his eyes, figuring it was easier to let his eyes adjust that way. Rome reached up and tugged on his arm.

"Rei," she said.

"Yeah, I'll be OK. I just need a minute to let my eyes adjust," Rei replied.

"REI!" Rome said, insistently.

"What?"

Even though his eyes were blurry from the brightness, Rei blinked a few times until his vision cleared.

There standing at the base of the ramp was an angry-looking mob holding spears, pole-axes, machetes, crossbows, swords, maces, clubs and knives plus a variety of other harsh-looking objects that Rei did not recognize. In summary, they were pointing pretty much every weapon ever conceived by primitive man at the space-faring couple.

"Great," Rei muttered. "From the frying pan into the fire."

Chapter 2

HANDS RAISED, REI WAITED PATIENTLY FOR SOMEONE TO SAY something. He figured if they were going to kill them, they would probably have done it already. A man in the front of the crowd took one step forward. "Nis nei damis nanhume croence equo. Berde," the man said in a peculiar dialect.

Rei leaned to his left and spoke to Rome quietly in English. "What children? Who are these people?"

"Shh..." Rome said. She pointed to her stomach.

"We are not after your children," she said in Vuduri. "As you can see, I am with child myself."

"Then who are you?" the man asked.

"I am Rome, this is Rei," replied Rome, pointing to the love of her life. "We are mandasurte, not Vuduri."

The people nearest the front gasped.

"This is not possible," said the man. "How do you come to fly a ship? You know the penalty is death."

"We are not from Deucado. We came from the Tabit system, 21 light years from here." She pointed straight up. "We did not know the law here. We were given this ship and another like it by the Vuduri to tow a cargo vessel here." Rome looked around then back at the man. "Did you see where it came down? Can you show us where it is? We need to inspect it."

"How do we know you are mandasurte?" the man asked skeptically. "You look Vuduri. You fly in a Vuduri ship. You could simply be spying on us."

"We are mandasurte, I assure you," Rome insisted.

"Prove it," said the man.

"Is it not sufficient that we are speaking?"

"No. That is not proof. There are many Vuduri who know how to speak."

"Then how? How do I prove it?"

"You decide," said the man through gritted teeth.

Rome lowered her head and looked him in the eye. "I will show you."

She turned toward Rei and, in English, she said, "Kiss me."

"What?" Rei whispered, confused.

"Kiss me like you love me," she insisted.

"But I do love you," Rei replied.

"Then do it!" Rome commanded.

"OK," Rei said. He opened his arms up to her and she entered them, pressing her belly up against him. He kissed her long and hard, not knowing why and after a moment or two, not really caring. He never tired of this woman, her soft skin, her clean smell, he just wanted to hold her always.

"Enough!" said the man. "This is very touching, but it proves nothing. I would not put it past our oppressors, even this. So you have learned to act. There may still be a purpose to your arrival that will spell pain for us. I do not think we should take a chance."

The crowd started murmuring and pushing forward. Some of them were raising their weapons and brandishing them about in a very menacing way. Rei started thinking furiously about some way to defend himself and Rome. Beyond hurling a chunk of ice at them, nothing came to mind. Worse, they had no weapons on board. He pushed Rome behind himself, using his body as a shield. Not that that would protect her but it was all he could think of at the moment.

"I will vouch for her," issued a voice from the back. All heads turned to look at the person who spoke. A silver-haired man worked his way forward and broke through the front lines.

"Aiee! I cannot believe it! Beo!" Rome shouted. She stepped around Rei and ran or perhaps waddled would be a better word, down the ramp and rushed into the man's arms.

"Beo?" Rei whispered to himself. "Father?"

Rome had buried her face in her father's chest with her arms locked around him. In turn, her father hugged her as tightly as he could given her condition. They held onto each other for the longest time, rocking back and forth. Finally, Rome pulled her head back and looked up into her father's eyes.

"You have been gone so long. We thought we had lost you forever," Rome whispered, tears of joy gushing down her face.

"My little Rome," said Fridone, "I, too, thought I would never see you again. You said you are mandasurte now?"

"Oh, Beo," she said, laughing and crying at the same time, "I have missed you so much and yes, I was Cesdiud."

"And you do not care?"

"I am happy beyond measure."

"Then I am happy for you. Oh, my little girl!" Fridone starting crying as well.

They hugged again, Rome's huge stomach pressing against him. After a few minutes, he pushed her away to regard her.

Rome ran her hand through her father's hair. "Beo, your hair. It has gotten so gray!"

"Yes, I have changed," replied Fridone somberly. Then he brightened up. "And speaking of changes, I see you have been busy," he said with a chuckle. Rome turned and pointed to Rei who walked down the ramp to stand beside the reunited pair, a bit wary of the cutlery around him.

"Beo, this is Rei. He saved me and perhaps the whole world. He is mau emir and the father of our child."

Fridone reached out with his arm and Rei extended his. Fridone grabbed a hold of it in a peculiar way and pulled him down toward him and gave him a hug, which Rei allowed. Then Fridone pushed him back and turned to Rome. "He is mandasurte, also? He certainly does not look like a Vuduri."

Rome nodded then said, "He is not Vuduri. He is from Garecei Ti Essessoni…"

Fridone jumped back reflexively, recoiling at Rome's words. Behind him, the people within earshot gasped. Rome ignored their reactions. She put her arm around Rei's waist and pulled him closer.

"He is not a killer," she continued. "He saved all of our lives."

Even as she spoke, the people behind muttered on. "Essessoni," they said among themselves. They whispered. Rei could hear them say things like "we are lost" and "murderers" in the background.

Trabunel, the man in front who had addressed them before, came over to them. "Is this true? Is that what was in your vessel over there?" He pointed to the woods behind them. "Did you bring the Erklirte among us?"

“I brought my people,” Rei said, in Vuduri. “But they are not what you think. We are just ordinary men like you. We were coming to this world to live free, like you.”

The man spat. “We are not free,” he said. “We live under the thumb of the Overmind here. We are prisoners of this world. We are the Ibbrassati, the oppressed.”

“Prisoners,” Rome asked. “What…”

Her question was interrupted by another man who came over and whispered into the first man’s ear. After the brief conference was over, Trabunel waved his hand to the crowd and spoke loud enough for all to hear.

“I believe that you are mandasurte, daughter of Fridone. No Vuduri could say those things or act like you do and be otherwise. As for you, Essessoni, we must hide your ship and your cargo vessel. Then we must get away from here. The Vuduri will be on their way and if they find your craft, they will take it. If they find you, they will kill you.”

Trabunel turned toward his men. “We must hide this ship and the other,” he shouted. “There is no heat signature to worry about. We only need camouflage. Use the nets. Elon, take some men and go find the Erklirte or whatever they are. Hide them as well.”

With murmurs of assent, the crowd began to disperse, some toward the tug, some in the opposite direction, deeper into the woods. Trabunel charged forward, away from the landing area. Fridone put his arm around his daughter and started guiding her away from her ship, in the same direction as Trabunel. Rei stood there and watched as the Ibbrassati swarmed over his tug, still caked in ice, laying netting over the top along with leaves, branches and other pieces of camouflage. Within a matter of minutes, his ship blended into the background so well that he had trouble picking it out himself. Amazed, he broke his concentration and hurried to catch up to Rome and her father.

The cane-tree forest was made up of thin reed-like trunks, almost like bamboo, most not more than four inches in diameter. Occasionally, there was one thicker. The very tops of the trees were a bright yellow while the lower leaves were yellow-green. The star Tau Ceti was more orange than Sol and so whatever passed for chlorophyll on this planet was skewed toward the lower frequencies in the electromagnetic spectrum. The colors reminded Rei of a really nice day in the fall, when the leaves were just beginning to turn. But the weather here was not consonant with that. In fact, it was fairly warm and somewhat humid.

They walked along a trail through the forest for a while. In many places, the trees had grown so thick that the sky overhead was hidden, mimicking nightfall. Eventually, they started down a steep winding path into a gorge that was hidden by a canopy of overhanging cane-trees. Fridone helped Rome navigate her way down, steadying her with his arm under her shoulder. They reached the base of the gorge but traveled only a short distance before Rome stopped. She was breathing heavily and bent over. Rei rushed over to her and knelt down on one knee to look up at her.

"Sweetheart," he said in English. "Are you OK?"

She gave him a half-smile. "You said you wanted to take a long walk when we first landed, right?" She winked at him.

Rei laughed but then the smile left his face. "Tell me, how do you feel?"

"Pregnant. Very pregnant." She went back to breathing heavily.

Rei shook his head and in one quick motion, scooped her up in his arms. His knees almost buckled and it took him a moment to right himself.

"You do not need to do this, mau emir. I will be all right," Rome said.

"It's OK, honey. I've been exercising for a year. I'm ready for this."

Fridone looked at him with a concerned expression but nodded slowly. Rei took one halting step, then another then another. After Rome could see that he was able to carry her, she put her arms around his neck and nestled her head against his shoulder.

"How far?" Rei asked Fridone, in Vuduri, slightly panicked.

"It is only about one-half kilometer from here," Fridone replied, pointing toward Trabunel who was some distance ahead. Fridone turned and started walking and Rei followed him. After they had gone only a short distance, Fridone stopped to let him catch up and placed his hand behind Rei's back. He helped Rei walk as best as he could.

"How did you know where to find us?" Fridone asked. "We have always been so careful to keep this enclave hidden. No one comes here. Our real settlement is about 40 kilometers to the south and west on the shores of Lake Eprehem. When the Vuduri come to take the children, they always do it well away from here."

"We did not know," Rei said, inhaling deeply. "We just jumped down here. MINIMCOM picked the spot." Rei took a quick breath. "MINIMCOM! Please, did you see where the Ark came down? Did you see our other tug?"

"I did not see either," Fridone replied. "We were out on patrol and heard a howling wind overhead. None of it made sense. We looked up and saw a black hole in the middle of the sky over the forest and something very large emerged. We saw your craft break free and fly toward us. We assumed it was the Vuduri who had found us. We were prepared to kill them if we had to. I am glad it was you. As far as your Ark is concerned, Trabunel seemed to know where your people landed though."

"We do not have that much time," Rei said. "We have to start thawing them out. Their freezing chambers are meant to be in space, not in this kind of heat. We have to thaw them out so they get reanimated properly. We cannot wait forever," he said.

"I understand," Rome's father replied. "We will tell Trabunel about this when we get to camp. We will help you with your people but we must be careful to avoid doing anything that will tip the Vuduri to our location first."

"OK," Rei said in English and he went back to concentrating on carrying the woman he loved and his unborn child to safety. He counted the steps silently and when he got to 1000, he flashed back to those lonely last minutes at Skyler Base, on Dara, when he thought he had lost Rome forever. But she was here and she was in his arms. He squeezed her tighter and they moved on.

They made their way along some rocks, following an intricate series of switchbacks, under some overhangs and finally entering a cave. Several men stood sentry duty outside while Fridone, Rei and Rome followed the leader within. Once they were inside, Rei heard a rumbling noise and turned to see them covering the hole with a large boulder and smaller ones.

Rei turned back and followed Fridone as he led the way deeper into the cave. After passing through some tunnels, they came to a sizeable cave with racks and racks of storage. The racks themselves were made of cane-tree wood. On them rested weapons, blankets and other paraphernalia. They entered a tunnel on the far side and continued on a downward slope, deeper and deeper into the mountain. The temperature dropped noticeably.

At last they got to a huge cavern. Rei looked up and could barely see the ceiling. All around them were tunnels and smaller caverns.

Fridone stopped and saw Rei looking up. "We call this 'The Cathedral,'" he said, "although what we worship, I do not know. Our living area is just ahead," he said and he waved his arm.

Rei followed Fridone to the right, through another tunnel into a small cave that had flimsy-looking bunk beds around the outskirts, stacked three tall, and a roaring fire in the middle. There were men and women there, most of whom looked older.

Fridone motioned to them. "Come sit by the fire and we will talk."

Rei set Rome down on the ground and the two of them went to the far side of the fire. He helped her strip out of her pressure suit while Fridone dragged some mats and some blankets over to make a soft place for Rome to recline. Rei joined her and she leaned up against him heavily. Trabunel came over and offered them water and an assortment of food which Rome gratefully accepted. This far along in her pregnancy, she was always ravenous.

Trabunel took a seat next to Fridone on the other side of the fire.

Rei was less interested in the food. "Can you tell us what is going on?" he asked. "None of this makes any sense."

Rome stopped eating to interrupt him. "Before you get into that, there is something I must know." She turned to face her father. "Beo, why did you leave us? Mea and I were devastated."

"How *is* your mother?" Fridone asked, ignoring her question.

"She is as well as can be expected. I know that she misses you. Life was never the same after you were gone."

Fridone's breath caught. He wiped away a tear. "I miss her, too," he said quietly. "I miss her so much. I feel like a part of me is gone. All the time. Even after all these years."

"So Beo, why did you come here? Why did you leave us?" Rome asked plaintively.

"Oh, my little Rome," Fridone replied gently. "I did not leave upon my own volition. I was kidnapped and brought here. We all were."

"Kidnapped," Rome exclaimed, horrified. "How? Why?"

"The why, I cannot answer. As for how, in my case, we were onboard our research vessel. We had departed Berlis Harbor and were out to sea to the south of the big island. Our ship was boarded by strange Vuduri."

"Strange?" Rei interjected. "What made them strange?"

"For one thing," continued Fridone, "they were harsh, even evil, with absolutely no hint of humanity about them. They were like living machines." Fridone pointed to his temple. "And their eyes!"

"What about their eyes?" Rome asked.

"They were not like a regular Vuduri. Their eyes were dark, no reflection," replied Fridone. "They had no life to them. I can only describe them by telling you these men had dead eyes."

"Vuduri with dead eyes? I have never seen such a thing. Why would they do this? Why would they kidnap you?"

"As I said, we do not know," he replied. "They never explained their motives to us. They rounded us up, herded us aboard a spaceship, transported us here and left. That is how most of the Ibbrassati arrived here. There are some fools about who willingly came here believing they were migrating to a new world but now they are just as much prisoners as we are."

"Why would they do such a thing?" Rome asked. "The Vuduri are all about efficiency. To force you to come here is the opposite of efficient."

Trabunel interjected, "Nothing about their behavior makes sense. The only thing we can think of is that they are trying to reduce the mandasurte population on Earth. Perhaps their hope is to one day cleanse the Earth of all mandasurte."

"Does anyone ever resist them?"

"Who would know? I would assume that if they resisted, they would just kill them outright."

"Why would they do that, sir?" Rei asked. "From what Rome tells me, the mandasurte keep to themselves…"

"We did," Fridone replied, picking up where Trabunel left off. "The Vuduri in charge of this world have no interest in justifying their plan to us. It is always the same. New mandasurte are brought here and none have any explanation as to why. The one thing our captors make clear to us is that we are not allowed access to Vuduri technology. They tell us it is a capital offense and we believe them."

"Why is that, Beo?" Rome asked. "What possible difference could it make to have access to technology?"

"We can only guess, Volhe," her father replied. "Clearly, Deucado is a prison world. Not one of us knew this. Access to technology might allow us to one day escape this planet and the Vuduri are determined to keep us trapped here. You cannot arm prisoners with the means to effect their release."

"They bring us here or they kill us," Trabunel said angrily, "it is that simple. Slowly but surely they will make all the mandasurte go away until there are no more left on the Earth."

"What about other worlds? What about Helome? There are many mandasurte that have left the Earth to go there. Yes?"

"Propaganda," Trabunel said. "Half-truth. They leave the Earth but they only end up here. Their ships are captured. No, our abductors will not stop until all the mandasurte are here."

"But I was connected. So was Mea. How could the Overmind keep such a secret?" Rome asked, completely puzzled.

"The only way is if the Overmind of Earth does not know. Somehow there must be a separate samanda, or perhaps a samanda within the samanda."

"That is not possible," Rome sputtered.

"You see that it is," Trabunel said. "There is a secret society on Earth, one that is hidden from ordinary Vuduri and mandasurte alike." Trabunel pounded his fist into his hand then grabbed it, shaking it at Rei and Rome. "They take us. They imprison us here. They rob us of our technology. There is no noble purpose here. Only evil," he said heatedly.

"If what you say is true, the very fabric of our society is at risk. It is not right. We…we need to tell them, tell the Vuduri of Earth, the normal ones. Beo, this cannot be allowed!" Rome said frantically.

"We have no way to get word back," replied Trabunel who was still agitated. "That is another one of the reasons why the Vuduri here do not allow us access to technology. They cannot take the chance that word gets back to Earth. Whoever is behind this wants to do this without anyone noticing. That is why they take the children."

"You mentioned that before," Rei said. "They take your children?"

"Not all of them. Only those that can connect to the Overmind. As soon as the child is born, if it is connected, the Vuduri begin to triangulate its position," said Trabunel. "They come for it very quickly. That is why we do not allow pregnant women to be anywhere near here. They must remain at the main settlement. We cannot have babies born here." He looked right at Rome who instinctively put her hand to her stomach.

"Why not? What's so special about this place?"

"Because we have some technology that we have stolen. And some that we are developing. We have a workroom and a forge back there." Trabunel jammed a thumb, pointing over his shoulder. "We cannot allow the Vuduri to find it. They would kill us. We are working on a way to make metals, materials, electronics and so forth. We will elevate ourselves back to our former technological level, even if it takes a hundred years."

"Metal?" Rei countered. "What about all the swords and knives that we saw earlier? There was nothing hidden about those!"

"Those are from the Vuduri. They give us the bare necessities to live. They just make sure that what they give us cannot be used against them."

"Could you not use a sword against one?" asked Rome. "Would it not wound or kill, just the same?"

"A sword is no match against a hand-weapon or energy projector," Trabunel spat out. "They are so convinced of their superiority that they do not fear such puny items."

"Puny, hah," Rei said. He pointed straight up. "They have no clue what is coming."

"What is coming?" Fridone asked. "What happened to you? Rome? Why are you here, anyway?"

Rome took a deep breath. "Beo, as I told you earlier, after you left, nothing was ever the same. Mea and I found dwelling among your family without you was too painful. We returned to I-cimaci to live."

"And then what?"

"I trained to become a lutteur and data archivist. And I was good at it. It was not a gaudy skill set but a necessary one. While you were gone, a star that was only 12 light years away from Earth disappeared. The Overmind sent out survey teams to investigate and I was selected for the team that was to go to Tabit. While we were there, one of our salvage crews came across Rei's Ark. That is how I met Rei."

"And his people, how do you know they are not the Erklirte?" Trabunel asked.

Rei started to speak but Rome interrupted. "If the Essessoni are anything like my Rei, they are good and decent and brilliant." She smiled up at him. "The one Ark that returned to Earth so long ago, the Erklirte, they were aberrant, perverted."

"We shall see," Trabunel said. "What happened to your mission? What did you find at Tabit?"

Rome recounted the story of shutting down the base prematurely, the starprobes, the Stareater and the VIRUS units. Trabunel and Fridone were incredulous. Rome also told them how OMCOM had planned his own escape and the subsequent mutations releasing who-knows-what into the universe.

"After you left, why did you come here? If you could tow the Ark, why not tow it back to Earth?" Trabunel asked.

"That question never really came up. I suppose it was because the Vuduri on Tabit wanted to help Rei complete his mission. And Deucado was his Ark's original destination," replied Rome.

"Or perhaps it was to isolate you," Trabunel pointed out. "You said you were Cesdiud. The two of you were mandasurte. You were carrying a ship full of mandasurte. Whoever is behind this, they did not want you on Earth. No, Deucado was the right place for you. They meant to send you here."

Rome frowned while she considered Trabunel's words. She shifted around, trying to get more comfortable. The pressure within her abdomen seemed so much greater now that they were in full gravity. Rei saw that she was having trouble and pulled her back so that more of her weight rested on him. This seemed to placate Rome, but only for a minute.

"I was part of the Overmind," Rome said harshly. "I would have known about such a plan. There were too few of us, only 80. We were too small for there to be a secret samanda among us. In fact, when the Overmind at Tabit sent us on our way, it loaded us up with as much equipment as possible. They gave us a molecular synthesizer, a memron fabricator and more. If they did not want us to have access to advanced technology, they would have not done that. No, the samanda that came to be on Tabit was not privy to the plan you described."

Rei spoke up. "So the Vuduri from Tabit send us here to live yet the Vuduri here want us dead? That must have been what Estar meant." Rei said in English. "Maybe the rest of you didn't know but she certainly did. That must have been why she tried to kill me."

"I do not see how," Rome answered. "The Overmind on Earth could not know what is going on here. And the people here do not know about the Stareaters. It is a good thing we have MINIMCOM and…" Rome's eyes widened. She turned to her father and said in Vuduri, "Beo, we have to get to the other tug. It is carrying the most important piece of equipment of all."

"And my people, we have to start thawing them before it is too late," Rei pointed out.

Fridone turned to Trabunel and said, "The Garecei Ti Essessoni. The reason they became the Erklirte is because they had powerful weapons…"

"Wait a minute," Rei interrupted. "We carry no weapons."

"Very well," said Fridone, "their technology, then. It might give us the edge we need to defend ourselves and declare our independence."

Trabunel put his fist to his mouth. They could see he was weighing the option. He exhaled forcibly and then nodded. He turned to Rei.

"Fridone is right. We will help you thaw your people."

"Thank you, sir," Rei exhaled.

"Rei, help me up," Rome said. She held out her hand. He leaned over and pressed his hand against her shoulder, pushing her back.

In English, he said, "Sweetheart. You can't go. You have to stay here."

"But, but…" she protested. "I can still walk."

"There's no way you can make it up to the Ark and back and there isn't anything for you to do, anyway. I can handle it."

"What about MINIMCOM? What about the other tug?" Rome asked, her voice catching.

"I'll check it out. I'll come back and let you know what's up. Don't worry about it."

"But I do not want to be apart from you. I am afraid."

"You'll be safe here," Rei responded. "These people will take care of you."

Rome tried to take a deep breath. "You are right. I will not argue." She switched to Vuduri. "Beo, while you are out there, please watch over him. Everything here is new to us."

"We will," Fridone replied. "Come, Rei, we must change your clothes. The ones you are wearing will give you away, should we be caught."

Rome barked out, "Caught?"

Rei said, "It'll be OK, Romey. I promise."

"You be careful, Rei Bierak. You come back to me. Aason and I need you."

"Aason?" he inquired.

She pointed to her stomach.
"Oh! Aason," he said, nodding. "I like it."

Chapter 3

A WARNING SIGNAL ORIGINATING FROM THE MIDAR ARRAY located on the far side of the planet was their first indication that something unusual was happening . The Overmind directed Pegus, the gray-haired leader of the Vuduri on Deucado, to activate the large view screen built into his workstation which also served as his desk. Standing directly behind Pegus was his most recent liaison from Earth, a woman named Sussen. Sussen, along with several of her strange Vuduri companions, had arrived on Deucado six months ago and brought with them information regarding the events on Tabit.

The flat panel display lit up relaying the instrumentation readout. At first, the dot on the screen was only a pixel or two wide but as it grew, Pegus could see it extending and elongating as it approached the planet. His eyes widened when the Overmind informed Pegus of its likely origin.

"Are you certain?" Pegus asked silently. *"It is too soon."*

"Look at the form factor," Sussen interjected into his mind. *"It is not a standard Vuduri starship."*

"You told us it was going to take nearly two years," Pegus protested. *"How could it have arrived here so quickly?"*

"I detect no PPT transceiver emanations from the craft," said the Overmind. *"Contact the vessel and confirm its origin. That will eliminate any speculation."*

Pegus pressed a few keys on the input surface built into his desk. The MIDAR display on the screen was replaced by the image of a Vuduri woman.

"Who are you?" he asked. "We do not detect any PPT resonance."

"We are mandasurte," the woman answered. "We have come from the Tabit stellar observatory. We are towing one of the lost Essessoni Arks that we found there."

This was the only confirmation he required. In a flat voice, Pegus replied, "On this world, mandasurte in possession of Vuduri technology is a capital crime. You have condemned yourself. You will die."

With that, he cut off contact.

"You know what to do," the Overmind stated.

Pegus nodded. Immediately, he scrambled a fleet of fighters to intercept the craft. The ancient spaceship was located on the far side of the planet so it would take them a little while to reach it but Pegus was not worried. The Essessoni vessel was simply too large to travel quickly. Despite the fact that it had arrived early, it still had taken the craft nearly a year to travel a distance that a normal starship would have traversed in just under two months.

As the blip on the MIDAR screen continued to grow, it was easy to see that the ship was very long and not very wide. His fighters would have no trouble at all taking it out. As he stared at his viewscreen, Pegus noticed that the ship was rotating around until it was pointing toward the planet. While he did not know their intentions, it meant they were trying something. He ordered the lead fighter to increase their plasma thrusters to the max to get to their quarry as quickly as possible.

Shortly thereafter, the MIDAR mounted in the nose of the fighter was returning a better image than the ground-based sensors so Pegus switched his main display to relay its information. Incredibly, the vessel ahead was becoming shorter. The only possible explanation was that it was entering a PPT tunnel. Pegus harshly commanded the fighter to fly even faster; however, the proximity projection revealed that his interceptor was not going to arrive in time. The Essessoni vessel grew smaller and smaller until it disappeared completely.

Pegus hissed a burst of air. He commanded the fighter to lift higher into orbit, perpendicular to where the tunnel had formed. This would establish a second point in space allowing them to plot the geometrical path of the jump. He instructed the remainder of his fleet to begin a parabolic spiral search on the opposite side of the planet along the vector formed between the two points.

Again and again, the Vuduri fighters jumped, each time farther out, following a geometrical path. They continued until they had covered a hemi-spherical region four light-seconds, nearly eight million kilometers, across.

Despite the immense distance, there was no sign of the Essessoni craft. Pegus knew its top speed. There was no way the craft from the past could had traveled even two light-seconds away from Deucado, let alone four. It had simply disappeared.

Pegus slammed his open palm against his desk. Even though the Vuduri do not normally express much emotion, the Overmind was clearly displeased that they had lost the ship and Pegus was taking the brunt of it.

Sussen stepped forward and pointed to the display. Silently, she communicated to Pegus, *"Play back the video recording from the lead ship."*

He considered questioning how that would help but he complied. He pressed a few keys on his input surface and the video started playing.

"Zoom in," she thought.

Pegus pressed a function key and the central section enlarged until their target nearly filled his screen. It was very blurry and the camera had a poor angle but he could see from the geometry that his suspicions were confirmed.

"They clearly jumped through a PPT tunnel," he thought. *"So why could we not locate their ship along the jump vector?"*

"You have made an assumption that I believe to be incorrect," she thought back to him.

"What assumption is that?"

"You assumed they jumped into space."

"Where else would they go?" he asked, confused. *"You are not thinking..."*

"Yes," Sussen interjected. *"They jumped down to the planet."*

"Impossible!" thought Pegus. He looked up at her face as she was leaning over his shoulder. Sussen and her comrades were strange, very much unlike an ordinary Vuduri, almost as if they were a different breed. Her eyes were two different colors and one did not have the reflective tapetum characteristic of all Vuduri. That eye looked almost black. It was just one small part of the whole package that made this woman unusual. However, Pegus refused to consider it any further because he knew she was reading his mind.

"There," Sussen thought, pointing. *"Look at the sections of the airfoils that got sheared off as it passed through the tunnel."*

"What about them?"

"There is light reflecting off of them. If they were jumping into space, that would not happen. Pan the image."

Pegus obeyed by pressing another key.

"Observe the space around the airfoils. You see that cloud of debris? It came from within the tunnel. That could only be material from the ground, not from space."

"You cannot form a stable PPT tunnel within a gravity well," he protested.

The Overmind of Deucado spoke up. *"The operative word in your statement is stable. The tunnel only needed to stay open for a short time. Always remember, if you eliminate the impossible, whatever remains, no matter how improbable, must be the truth. I agree with Sussen. They jumped down to the planet."*

Pegus shook his head. He was not going to fight with the Overmind. He silently recalled his fleet and commanded them to return to the planet to begin a world-wide search.

"Do not bother," the Overmind said. *"We can deduce exactly where they went."*

In his mind, the Overmind showed Pegus the precise spot where the ship must have landed, the Ibbrassati enclave in the forest to the north of their settlement.

Pegus was incredulous. *"How could you know this?"* he asked. *"How would they know to land there? They have never been to this planet before. They do not even know the true purpose of Deucado. How could they possibly know about the Ibbrassati's secret enclave? It would have to be an incredible coincidence."*

"There is no such thing as a coincidence," the Overmind declared.

Pegus took a deep breath then said, *"Very well. I accept your assertion. I will send my fleet to that exact location and destroy them."*

"No," countered the Overmind. *"You will do nothing. We need that base to continue operation. Just wait."*

"What about the Essessoni? Are we to let them run free?"

"Of course not," Sussen replied firmly. *"But you do not understand the Essessoni. The Overmind is correct. All you have to do is wait."*

"Wait for what?" Pegus asked.

REBELLION

"Wait and they will come to us."

Chapter 4

THE STAR, TAU CETI, WAS ALREADY SETTING AS REI, FRIDONE, Trabunel and a cohort of men exited the cave. Very quickly, it became so dark that Rei could barely see the way ahead. As they marched forward, Rei found that it actually seemed easier to walk with his eyes closed, a condition that made no sense. He just concentrated on following Fridone and not falling. They emerged from the gorge and reentered the cane-tree forest.

"Rei, you must be on alert here," Fridone said. "There are some animals that can hurt you if you are not careful."

"What kind? What do they look like?"

"They are not like animals from Earth. They do not have distinct form. They are more like living cloth or blankets. They are slow but they are strong. Sometimes, they climb the trees…" Fridone pointed up. "They sit up there and if you walk underneath, they drop onto you. The larger ones are big enough to completely cover you up. They can suffocate you and then eat you in tiny, tiny pieces. Do you see the poles there?"

Fridone pointed to some men in their hunting party that had tall sticks shaped like gaffes. Rei squinted but could not see anything.

"They watch for the 'falling blankets.' They move them, they can pull them off. If you are paying attention, you will not be in any danger. They are very slow. If you are with someone, you will be all right."

"Are there any other kinds of animals besides these falling blankets? Intelligent ones? Like us?" Rei asked.

"No. The indigenous wildlife here is limited to variants of blankets and some creatures that swim."

"Why so limited?"

"We do not know," Fridone answered. "It must have something to do with the environment but we have not studied it. There have been stories about other types, animals that are intelligent. They supposedly live deeper in the woods. But I have been here for ten years. I have never seen even one. I think they are just stories."

The small group reached a clearing. "Look," Fridone said, pointing ahead. Very low on the horizon to the west was a bright reddish-orange shape, distorted to look almost like an egg. “Mockay,” Fridone said. “It rises.”

“Sleek,” Rei replied in English. Fridone moved away rapidly and took the lead and Rei followed him, winding their way through the cane trees and bush until they came to another, much larger clearing. Scrutinizing the area, Rei realized it was not a clearing at all. It was his Ark! The lead men were already pulling away the camouflage. He worked his way along the side, lifting the netting as he went until he came to the lattice that separated the huge cargo section from the personnel section. Continuing to the very front, in the dim light of the tiny moon, Rei saw a sight that made his heart sink. Protruding from beneath the crew section of the Ark was a small part of the underbelly of MINIMCOM’s shuttle. The rear stabilizer was bent sideways and only about 15 feet of the cargo section was visible. The cargo hatch was open and lying flat on the ground. The cargo ramp had sprung open and was pointing in the air at an odd angle. The rest of MINIMCOM’s tug was buried underneath the Ark, smashed, as far as Rei could tell. From the geometry of the two vehicles, it looked like MINIMCOM had enough time to disengage from the Ark but that was all. He took a deep breath. The little computer had sacrificed his own life to save Rei, Rome and Rei’s people. Rei remembered that Rome had once said that OMCOM and his ilk were amoral. But this was a moral act - or at the very least a compassionate one.

Fridone came over to look over the wreckage with Rei.

“This was your other shuttle?” he asked.

“Yes,” Rei said, sadly.

“What was in there?”

“MINIMCOM.”

“A computer?” Fridone shook his head.

“He wasn’t just a computer,” Rei replied. “He…he was a friend. He took care of us.”

“I do not think he survived the fall,” Fridone said matter-of-factly.

“No.” Rei gulped. “I do not think he did.”

“What else did you have in this ship?”

"The VIRUS units, a memron fabricator and…oh no!" Rei shouted.

"What?" Fridone asked with concern in his voice.

"Captain Keller," Rei said in English. He got down on his hands and knees and crawled in between the cargo door and ramp. He breathed a sigh of relief when he saw the striped sarcophagus, still intact, secured in the section that was not crushed underneath the Ark.

"Help me pull this out," he shouted to Fridone in Vuduri.

Several men crawled in while others used brute strength to raise the cargo ramp high enough to allow the extraction of the sarcophagus. While it took four men including Rei, they were able to free the chamber and drag it out into the area next to the Ark.

"What do we do?" Fridone asked Rei.

"He looks to be still frozen," Rei said, inspecting the chamber. "We should probably take him back to the cave to wake him. When people are first thawed, they tend to be very weak. They will need some place to rest once the reanimation sequence is complete."

Fridone laughed sardonically. "They sleep for centuries and then they need to rest?"

"Pretty ironic, huh?" Rei said.

"Where are the rest of your people located?"

"I will show you."

With a little help, Rei was able to open the side hatch of the crew compartment and entered via the built in steps. He showed the men how to release the clamps, freeing the sarcophagi. They carried the first one out and set it next to Keller's sarcophagus.

"Can your men take that one first?" Rei asked, pointing to Keller's chamber. He turned to Fridone. "How are we going to work this?"

"You and I and Zander and Pilar will carry your striped one back. The others can bring the second. When we get back to the cave, we will send the next two teams up. That will keep our exposure to a minimum. We can bring back two at time. How many are there?"

"More than 500," Rei answered.

Fridone sighed. “It will take us a while but I believe we can get them all back before dawn. Let us proceed.”

The three men and Rei each grabbed a corner of the rail around Keller’s sarcophagus and lifted. Mockay was already setting in the east as they started along the trail leading back to the gorge. To its left, the other moon, Givy, was rising slowly, also in the east, and the two appeared almost as ships passing in the night. The tiny moon was just a sliver and wouldn’t provide much illumination at all, especially under the canopy of the cane-trees. In the waning glow of Mockay, Rei figured they’d get to the edge of the gorge before he effectively went blind again.

He was right. By the time they reached the edge, Mockay had settled and once again, Rei had to use starlight to see what he was doing. Givy was only a few arcseconds up and was really nothing more than a bright spot in the sky, hardly useful for illumination.

Traveling down the gorge was not as difficult as Rei imagined. They more or less slid the sarcophagus down the slope. By concentrating on the task at hand, he willed himself to ignore the fact that it was nearly impossible to see. At last, they got to the bottom of the path and the four men lifted the sarcophagus again. At this point, it was pitch black. As before, Rei closed his eyes again and as before, surprisingly, it seemed easier to walk. The others more or less pulled him along.

When they reached the cave, they had a little trouble getting the sarcophagus through the narrow entrance. Once inside, the team headed straight back through to The Cathedral.

“Can we set this down for a minute?” Rei asked.

“Of course,” Fridone replied. The other men complied.

Rei turned to his right and followed the tunnel to the area where he had left Rome. The mats and blankets were there, but no Rome. He scanned all around the cave and did not see her anywhere.

“Where is Rome?” he asked one of the women. She just shook her head and did not answer. She waved at Rei and he followed her a little deeper into yet another alcove off to the side. He entered and found Rome lying on an actual bed, with a cloth on her head and two women attending to her. He rushed to her bedside

“Rome, what’s going on?” he said in English.

She turned her head to look at him and gave him a weak smile. “Mau emir. I am fine. I just got a little faint. I think it is possible that baby Aason wants to join us early, though.”

Immediately, she grimaced and put her hands on her stomach. The women clucked over her and one patted her head with the cloth.

Trabunel came in from the other side and came over to Rei.

“You must move her out of here soon. We cannot take the chance that the baby is connected. If it is, they will find us here and all will be lost.”

“This is crazy,” Rei said. “You cannot move her now. Look at her. Plus, the baby is half mine. How can it be connected, anyway?”

“I do not claim to understand the genetics but his mother is Vuduri. That may be all that is required. We cannot take this chance. You will have enough time to show us how to thaw out your people. Then we will arrange for you to go to our settlement to the south. Our boats move very swiftly. The settlement is where the Vuduri expect us and if your child is connected, that will be acceptable if they come for him. He will have no knowledge of this place.”

“They’re not coming for my baby,” Rei said in English. Then in Vuduri, “Why do I have to let them?”

“They will take the baby,” Trabunel insisted. “They do not care if they take it with you alive or dead.”

“NO!” Rome exclaimed. “Not dead. Rei, you listen to him.”

“But sweetheart, I can’t let them take our baby,” he said in English.

“We will find a way, Rei. You will find a way. You always do.”

“All right. I understand,” he said. He took a deep breath. “Let me show them how to thaw my people out. Then I’ll come back and be with you, Romey.”

“Always, mau emir, always,” she said.

Rei kissed her and left the alcove and followed Trabunel back to where Fridone and Captain Keller’s dark gray sarcophagus sat. Once again, the four men lifted the sarcophagus and entered a side tunnel, traveling some distance until they came upon another cave, even larger than The Cathedral. The cave was completely empty, just some rocks scattered about its broken floor.

Fridone indicated the area in front of them. “This will be our staging area,” he said.

The cave was huge. Even in the flickering darkness illuminated by just a few torches, Rei could get a sense that it went deeper for hundreds and hundreds of meters. It was no wonder that the Ibbrassati picked this as their secret base. This complex of caves was capable of holding hundreds, if not thousands of people undetected.

They carried the sarcophagus to the far left and set it down. Rei waited for the men entering the cave came to stand around him. Eventually, the group amount to 20 or 30 people. Rei went around to the foot of the red-striped sarcophagus and waved them over. They formed a semi-circle around him, three men deep.

“Can you bring some torches over?” he asked.

Two men complied. Rei addressed them using as loud of a voice as he could muster.

“To initiate the reanimation sequence, all you need to do is rotate these two rods…”

Rei grasped the black ends of the radioactive rods using the integrated handles.

“You turn them until the triangle is pointing straight up.”

Rei rotated the left rod clockwise and the right rod counter-clockwise until the arrows embossed on the cap pointed upward.

After a few minutes, the hoarfrost that had collected on the outside of the chamber began to thaw. The needles on the dials above the knobs began to quiver and then slowly crept north as the nuclear fire penetrated the internal workings of the sarcophagus.

Rei pointed to the dials. “The rods are causing heat. That melts the ice.”

“Why do you need to do that?” one man asked. “Why not just let them thaw out naturally?”

“If we just them thaw on their own, they would drown or die,” Rei said. “The rods make the electricity that is needed to reanimate the person within using a pre-determined sequence. For example, after the fluid melts, the pump activates and drains it away. There is a…' He switched to English, "Defibrillator." Rei paused seeing the blank expressions around him.

"It is a device that restarts their heart," he said in Vuduri. Now the men nodded.

Rei continued, "After that, there is a blower to dry them off and warm them up."

He bent over and could see that the transparent cover was now completely clear.

"It is working!" Rei said excitedly. "Look!"

Several of the men bent over to peer into the chamber. They could see the face of the man frozen inside was visible, a breathing mask covering his nose and mouth. He lay beneath several inches of slushy light green ice.

As predicted, the ice eventually melted and a quiet whirring noise began. The liquid drained out of sight. Rei did not wait for the defibrillator to kick in. He showed the men gathered about how to retract the hood exposing Captain Keller to the outside air. They could hear the heater/blowers operating.

Even as the pumps were removing the last few liters of fluid, a high-pitched noise issued forth followed by a pop. Within the chamber, the body jumped slightly and the previously frozen man moved his head from side to side.

"As soon as you see they have been revived, you need to remove these two pads," Rei said, even as he was peeling the defibrillator leads back. "Most of the chambers will not have the breathing mask."

Captain Keller clenched his fists over his chest and started shivering. They could see his eyelids flicker as he tried to open his eyes. Luckily, the lighting in the cave was dim. Rei remembered how much the light hurt his eyes when he was first awakened.

Captain Keller coughed and thrashed and Rei showed the men how to retract the hood fully. They helped the newly thawed man to sit up and covered him in a blanket. He blinked and blinked, trying to make out his surroundings. Rei spoke to him in English.

"Captain Keller?"

"Yes," the man rumbled. His voice was rusty from disuse. "Who are you?"

"I am Rei Bierak, one of your engineers."

"Where are we?" the captain asked.

"We are in a cave on a planet called Deucado by the inhabitants. Deucado is the second planet out in the Tau Ceti system. We made it, sir!"

Captain Keller tried to look at him but he failed. His head fell down on his chest but it did not stop him from speaking.

"Why are you awake? The command crew is supposed to be reanimated first. And what are we doing on the ground? And how could the world be named already? We're the first people here," he said, exhaling his words more than speaking them.

"Sir, I know this will be hard for you to understand and we'll review it again later but it is the year 3588. We've been asleep for almost 1400 years. There have been people on this world for a long time before we got here."

Captain Keller lifted his head and squinted at Rei. "I have no idea what you're talking about. How could it be 3588? What are you saying? What the hell is going on?"

Rei stooped down so that Keller could see him. "Sir, we got knocked off course. We ended up 21 light years from our target. We only arrived here one day ago. I know it seems hard to believe and I'll explain everything to you but for now, just know that we are at Tau Ceti and the crew is being recovered as we speak. There's a lot you have to learn and I'll lay it all out for you when you are up to it."

Captain Keller's head began to list to the side. "I don't believe a word you're telling me but I'm too drugged to even think about it." Keller's eyes started to close. His next words came out barely louder than a whisper. "I've got to sleep now," he said.

"All right, sir. I understand. But let's get you dressed first," Rei said sympathetically.

Rei showed the men standing around how to unlock the storage compartment on the bottom. Within the vacuum-sealed compartment, they found a brown flight suit that they used to dress Captain Keller. Rei showed them the Velcro slippers and the baseball cap stored next to them.

After Keller was fully clothed, Rei spoke to him again. "Sir, these people will take you somewhere where you can get some rest. I'll come see you when you are feeling better."

"Whatever," Keller said, without much interest.

Two men lifted him up and placed his arms over their shoulders. Keller attempted to walk but in reality, the men mostly carried him off to another section of the cave.

"This is what you should expect from each of them," Rei announced in Vuduri. "It is difficult to find out that you are not where you thought you would be and everything you know about the world is wrong."

"Is every one clear on the procedure?" Fridone asked, looking around.

The men nodded in assent.

"We can do this, Rei" Fridone said. "Go see to Rome."

"Thank you, sir," Rei replied and he hurried off to her alcove. Rome's face lit up when she saw him enter the room.

"Mau emir," Rome said.

Rei sat by the edge of the bed. He took her hand in his and kissed it gently.

"What did you find?" she asked him. "What about MINIMCOM?"

Rei took a deep breath. "He's gone, sweetheart. His tug got smashed under the Ark."

"Oh no!" Rome cried out then she grabbed her stomach and said "Oh no!" again. After she recovered, she asked, "Are you sure?"

"I'm pretty sure," Rei answered grimly. "There was nothing left of the forward section and only a piece of the cargo hold."

"I am so sad," Rome said, shutting her eyes.

"Me too," Rei replied. "He was a good friend."

"And very brave."

"It was more than that, Rome."

"What do you mean?"

"He knew he had Captain Keller's sarcophagus in the back. It must have been his final act to swing the rear of the tug around so the sarcophagus didn't get crushed. MINIMCOM put himself directly under the Ark to save somebody he had never met."

"That is so like him," Rome said. "The machines…in some ways they are very different than us but in others, they are the same. What about your Captain? Did he survive?"

"Yes," Rei answered. "We've already thawed him out."

"You did? Is he all right?"

Rei cocked his head and shrugged. "About as good as I was when I first woke up. He's resting in the back. He was pretty disoriented."

"As were you, if you recall," Rome said with a smile, albeit a weak one.

"I still am, honey," Rei said, laughing gently. "I gave him the capsule summary of where we are and he didn't believe a word of it."

"You will teach him. You will teach all of them," Rome insisted.

"Sure."

Rome grimaced as another wave of pain washed over her. Rei kissed her hand again. "Can I do anything for you? Do you need anything?" he asked her.

"Not right now. I am doing the best I can. Paddy and Karin have been very good to me."

Rei turned and looked at the two women standing at the entrance of the alcove and they nodded to him.

"I told you they want us to move you," Rei said, worriedly. "Are you going to be able to make it?"

"I will have to, will I not?"

"I guess so," said Rei, unconvinced.

"It is so strange," Rome observed. "I no longer know what time it is, whether we should be awake or asleep. I do not even know where I am."

"I understand completely. I have no clue where we are either."

"But Rei?"

"Yes?" Rei responded.

"As long as I am with you, I do not care," Rome said.

Rei laughed. "Me neither, honey. Me neither."

"I think I am tired now."

"Do you want to rest some more?"

"Yes, I will, oh!" Rome cried out and doubled up in pain.

"What is it, sweetheart?"

"I, ow, ow, ow," Rome said. "I can't… breathe." She tried to take a breath but could not. She fell back, limply.

"Rome!" Rei shouted. He stroked her brow. "Rome!"

Rome opened her eyes but she was unable to focus. "Rei… This… is… not… labor."

In a panic, Rei looked up at one the women, Paddy, hovering nearby. "What kind of medical facilities do you have at your settlement?" he asked her.

"None really," Paddy answered, somewhat bitterly. "The Vuduri keep all the advanced equipment to themselves, inside their compound. They really do not care if we die. Of disease, an accident, in childbirth. It does not matter to them."

"Die!" Rei exclaimed. "Who said anything about dying?"

The woman pointed to Rome. "She is too big. Your baby does not fit inside her. This is why she is in so much distress."

Rei looked down at the woman he loved, suffering. Instantly, he knew what he had to do.

"Rome, I'm going to fly you to the Vuduri," he announced.

Paddy gasped. "You cannot do that," she said. "It is forbidden for mandasurte to have access to Vuduri technology. They will kill you."

"Not if they see Rome is pregnant," Rei replied.

"They only want children who are connected," said the other woman, Karin.

"Well if they want the children who are connected, it won't do them any good if they're dead. I can't take the chance. Romey?"

"Yes, mau emir," she said weakly.

"I'm taking you to the tug. We're going to fly into the lion's den."

"Yes, mau emir," she said. "Things cannot get any worse than they are now."

"I'll be back in a minute then. I have to go tell Trabunel and your father."

"Ow-ow," she said and closed her eyes. "Please hurry."

Rei raced back to where they were keeping Captain Keller. Fridone and Trabunel were standing next to his bed.

Rei spoke in Vuduri. "I have to fly Rome to the Vuduri compound. Otherwise, Paddy said she might die."

Fridone gasped.

Trabunel put his hand on Rei's arm. "You do realize they will most likely kill you," he said gravely.

"I know. But I cannot let Rome suffer. She is my whole world. If anything happened to her, I would die anyway. So…"

"What kind of gibberish is that?" Keller asked, even though his eyes were shut.

"It's their language. It's called Vuduri," Rei said in English. "I have to take care of Rome. She's carrying my baby and she's in pain. I have to take her to get medical help."

"Baby? How long have you been awake?" Keller asked.

"Over a year."

"Over a year?" Keller exclaimed, trying to open his eyes.

"Captain Keller, I'm sorry but I can't talk to you right now. Just stay here with these people and listen to them. There's a bunch of crazies out there who will kill you on sight. You have to lay low."

"What are you talking about?" the captain responded, trying to sit up. "Ow," he said, "my back."

"I don't have time to explain. You just have to trust me. These people, this cave, it's safe as long as you stay here. They're bringing the rest of our people in. They'll help you. But I have to go."

The three men left Keller sitting there even more confused than ever. On their way back to Rome's chamber, Rei stopped and regarded the two men.

"Can I ask you something?"

"What is it?" Trabunel asked.

"Yes?" Fridone chimed in.

Rei looked at him, then Trabunel then back to Fridone again. "Do you guys still have marriage?" Rei said the word in English. Neither Trabunel nor Fridone understood.

"Uh, civil union? A commitment?" Rei asked in Vuduri.

Fridone nodded, “When a couple loves each other and wants to commit, they pledge themselves to one another. It is called Cesa.”

“Is there any kind of ceremony? Is there a lot to it?”

“Yes, we have a ceremony,” answered Fridone. “There are a few elements but it is not fixed.”

“Then sir, I want to marry your daughter. Now. I want our son to be born into a proper family.”

“That is very kind of you, Rei,” said Rome’s father. “And to this, Rome agrees?”

“I have not asked her yet, sir. I did not even know if it was still done. How do you do it?”

Trabunel spoke up. “I am the leader. I can perform the ceremony. But if what you say is true, time is critical. The longer you wait, the longer Rome suffers. If you are going to do this, you should do it quickly. We will arrange for you to get a travois to carry Rome back to your shuttle.”

“Thank you.”

Trabunel went and flagged down some men. Fridone and Rei made their way back to Rome’s alcove. Rei sat down beside her.

“Romey?” he asked in English.

“Yes, mau emir?”

“We’re going to take you back to the tug and get you some help but, I wanted to know, um…uh,” Rei stuttered.

“What is it?”

Rei decided to sink to one knee. He took up Rome’s hand and looked into her glowing eyes and said in English, “Will you marry me?”

“Marry?” she asked, surprised.

“Cesa,” said Fridone.

Rome’s whole face lit up. “How sweet of you. Of course I will marry you. We will do this when we get back.”

“No, Rome. I want to do it now. I want Aason born with his parents married.”

“Why?”

“Because you never know what’s going to happen. I want Aason to grow up knowing his parents loved each other very much and that they were committed to one another.”

“I understand,” said Rome. “But we do not need to. Aason will know.”

“Honey, it’s something I need to do,” Rei insisted.

“If it is that important to you, so be it,” Rome said as Trabunel reentered the room.

The Ibbrassati leader spoke up. “There is usually a set of pledges and the families meet before the ceremony. It normally takes some time. But for you, we can eliminate this step. I can make it brief. We can do it right here, if you would like.”

“How does it work?” Rei asked.

“I will just ask the two of you to pledge your lives together. If you give your assent, you are bound. Your word is your bond. Understand?”

Both Rei and Rome nodded their head. The two women rushed over and helped Rome to stand. Rei took her arm and steadied her as they walked over to Trabunel. Rei put his left arm around her and with his right hand he reached down and took her hand. He raised it to his lips and kissed it gently.

They both looked up at Trabunel who asked, “Rei, do you give your word and pledge to stay by this woman’s side? To always honor and cherish her uniqueness? To be faithful, loving and truthful? Through the bad as well as the good, for as long as you live?”

Rei took her hand and kissed it again. “I do,” he said.

“And Rome, do you give your word and pledge to stay by this man’s side? To always honor and cherish his uniqueness? To be faithful, loving and truthful? Through the bad as well as the good, for as long as you live?”

Rome lifted Rei’s hand up to her lips and kissed it tenderly. “I do,” she said.

“Then you are now bound forever as husband and wife. And the best of luck to you always. I am very happy for you.” Trabunel turned and looked at Fridone. “And for you, too, Fridone,” he said.

Rome sidled around and put her arms around Rei’s neck. In turn, Rei put his arms around her waist and kissed her deeply. For just one moment, all was right with the world.

Fridone came over and hugged and kissed Rome. “You have my blessing, always.”

She looked up at him. “Beo?

“Yes, Volhe, I...”

“Ungh,” Rome said, and doubled over in pain.

Chapter 5

A SHORT WHILE LATER, TWO MEN ARRIVED CARRYING A TRAVOIS which was really nothing more than two long branches with a blanket secured between them. Rei helped his wife settle onto the blanket. He stood up and grabbed one end while Fridone took the other, treating it more as a stretcher.

Exiting the cave quickly, they made their way out of the gorge and through the cane-tree woods. Several of the men accompanying them stayed in front, carrying large gaffes, looking for 'falling blankets'.

As they made their way along the path, they were constantly being passed by groups of men ferrying the sarcophagi back to the cave. That continued until they came to the fork in the path that led back to the Flying House.

While it was not yet dawn, the sky in the east was brightening. Soon they were in the clearing where the tug had landed. Two of the men that had accompanied them pulled the netting and camouflage off of the ship while Fridone and Rei helped Rome stand up so she could walk up the ramp.

When they reached the top, Rei asked Rome in English, "Do you want to stay in the bedroom?"

"Much as I would like to, I do not think you should fly this alone. I will sit in the cockpit for as long as I can."

"OK," he said. They made their way forward, into the cockpit and got her as comfortable as possible in the co-pilot's seat.

"Hold on just a second," Rei said. He raced back to the galley and returned carrying a white bottle. He handed the bottle to Fridone.

"What is this?" Fridone asked.

"Every one of my people will have terrible back pain once they can stand. Please give one of these pills to each of them. That will get them healthy fairly quickly."

Fridone took the bottle from him. "I will see to it."

Rei sat down and buckled himself into the pilot's chair. Fridone bent over and kissed his daughter on her forehead.

"You be careful, my daughter. You come back to me with my grandson. There is much that I want to teach him."

"I will, Beo. I will do my best."

Fridone worked his way around to Rei and put his hand on his shoulder.

"You take care of my daughter, son. She is the most precious thing in all the world."

"Yes, she is," Rei replied. "I will take care of her." He indicated forward. "Now which way do we go?"

"You must head south first and until you reach our settlement on the lake. Take a wide berth and come back around. That way, if you are spotted, there will be no undue curiosity about our encampment here."

"How do I do that?" Rei asked.

"Follow the stream in front of you to the south until you come to where it merges with the river Karole," replied Fridone. "You follow the river all the way until it empties into Lake Eprehem. Our main settlement sits on the eastern shore. Once you are past the village you can circle around and then head due east. I do not know how fast your ship flies so I cannot tell you how long it will take. All I can tell you is that the Vuduri compound is located somewhere along the coast. Perhaps a bit north once you get to the ocean. I know nothing more."

"Thank you. I guess we will figure it out when we get there."

"Very well. Good luck to the two of you," Fridone said and after kissing his daughter once more, he left.

Rei closed the cargo door and ramp using the front console. After a cursory checkout, he pulled back on the throttle and the EG lifters pushed the craft into the air. He did a quick test, cycling the now-thawed landing gear. All appeared in order. Rei drifted to the west slowly using MIDAR to search the ground until he found the stream. He turned the ship and traveled along the stream almost due south until it joined a much wider, fast-moving river. They picked up a little speed while following the river southwest. Soon, they came upon a village, easily recognized by the smoke and haze from the numerous fires there. Rei banked around the village and hovered over the lake.

"Which way do we go?" Rei asked.

"Beo said to head east, Rome said, pointing at the rosy orange ball, just coming over the tops of the trees. "The sun rises in the east on this planet just like on Earth."

"OK," Rei said, "here we go."

Rei pulled back on both sticks to gain altitude, then leveled off and turned until they were pointing right toward the sun. He edged the right control stick forward and they began their cross-country journey.

"How do we find them?" he asked Rome as they flew over seemingly endless stretches of cane-tree woods.

"I do not know," Rome answered. "However, the Vuduri are very practical people. They would build their outpost near the coast, perhaps by a bay. Let us travel along this vector until we hit the ocean. We will use the sensors to see if we can find signs of their enclave once we get there."

"Roger that," Rei said.

"And stay low. There is no sense in letting them know we are coming before we have to. Ungh" Rome grabbed her stomach again.

Rei dipped down slightly then leveled off. He punched the plasma thrusters, easing them up slowly to minimize the stress on Rome. When they gained sufficient velocity, he eased off on the thrusters and propelled the ship forward using the EG pods only.

"Romey, what do we do when we get there? Any ideas on how to keep them from killing us as soon as they see us?"

"I do not know. We will have to figure that out when the time comes," Rome replied.

"What's our cover story? What about the Ark?"

Rome thought about it for a moment. "We will say that the Ark burned up and fell into the lake and sank to the bottom."

"OK," Rei said. "But how do we explain my clothes?"

Rome's face grimaced in pain. "I do not know," she said sharply. "I cannot think about such things right now."

"OK, honey," Rei said, knowing that it was the pain talking to him harshly.

Haltingly, Rome took in a deep breath as best as she could and then let it out slowly. "I am going to close my eyes now," she said. "Wake me when we get close."

"Sure, sweetheart. You rest."

Then, Rei heard her say in Vuduri, "*He is so good to me. I really love him.*"

"I love you too, honey," Rei replied, not really looking at her.

"What?" Rome said, opening her eyes. "I did not say anything. But I do love you."

"OK, whatever you say, sweetheart."

"*He is so strange sometimes.*"

Rei laughed and turned to look at her. Her eyes were closed. He just shrugged it off.

After an hour or so, off in the distance, he could see the twinkling of the huge bay that led to the eastern ocean.

"Romey," he said softly.

She opened her eyes and smiled at him and then frowned again. She peeked over the windshield then looked down at the instruments.

"That way," she said, pointing to Rei's left. Rei reduced their speed and then banked the tug left and started to follow the edge of the bay north. Rome played with the sensors. She found an anomalous reading at the tip of the bay, perhaps 50 kilometers to the north, so they figured that was where the Vuduri lived.

The proximity detectors went off. The onscreen displays changed to MIDAR and two blips appeared, approaching rapidly. They looked out the window and saw two spacecraft heading right for them. The two ships came at them fast and only veered off at the last second. No shots were fired from the warcraft but they came around behind them and settled in just to the left and right of their wings.

The video display lit up and they looked down to see the same Vuduri man who had addressed them when they first arrived.

"Why are you coming here?" the man demanded in Vuduri. "I told you we must kill you for possession of illegal technology."

Rome spoke up. “This ship was given to us by the Vuduri stationed at Tabit. We have no use for it. We simply wanted to return it to its rightful owner. That is hardly an offense worthy of death.”

Rei watched his wife as she continued. “In addition, I am with child. I will need medical supervision. I come from Vuduri stock. The child may be connected. If he is, I want him integrated into the Overmind immediately.”

Rome tried to take a breath. “You would not take that opportunity away from a newborn. We need your help. It is that simple. You need not do anything hasty. After all,” Rome said with a dramatic pause, “you can always kill us later.”

“Where are the Erklirte?” the man demanded.

“The Ark was destroyed upon reentry. It sunk to the bottom of the lake. This tug is the only thing that survived.”

Rei looked at his wife, lying with the best of them. He was impressed.

“Very well,” said the man. “The fighters will escort you to our settlement. Do not try anything foolhardy or we will be forced to shoot and I promise you we will not miss.”

“You heard the man,” Rome said, sotto voce. “Follow the fighters and do not fool around.”

“Yes, ma’am!” Rei said. Then in English, “You are pretty awesome, you know.”

“Yes, I am,” she replied. She closed her eyes and put her hands on her stomach. “I wish this would stop. And soon.”

“We’re on our way,” Rei replied.

They traveled north following the coastline until they came to a small inlet. The fighters banked inland and Rei followed them until they came to the Vuduri compound, which consisted of some towers and a few low-lying buildings. They flew past, heading west until they reached a medium-sized spaceport. The fighters guided them to a large paved-over area to the north of the main terminal. They landed well apart from the other ships. Rei opened all the airlocks and the cargo ramp. Very carefully and very slowly, he helped Rome walk past the cargo hold and down the ramp. At the bottom stood a group of Vuduri carrying weapons.

“I thought the Vuduri were non-violent,” Rei said in English, “they don’t look too peaceful to me.”

“This is all so wrong,” Rome replied, shaking her head.

The soldiers escorted them across the tarmac. All around them were other ships, some larger, some smaller. Rei spotted the tops of the towers way off in the distance. He didn’t know how Rome was going to make it. To his relief, even as they were walking, a vehicle pulled up, sort of an oversized flying golf cart and they were herded into the back seat. A soldier sat on either side of them with two more in the front. They traveled down a semi-paved road, winding their way toward the compound.

Eventually, they were driven to what appeared to be the front gate. The surrounding walls must have been three meters tall and were made out of a foam-like material reminiscent of Skyler Base.

At the gate, other guards inspected them, but in typical Vuduri fashion, not a word was spoken. Finally the gate opened and they entered the compound.

Rei was shocked to see lush gardens, fountains, flowers, and even statues. The edifice and its surroundings reminded him of a Roman palace. The front door had columns. Overall, it was actually quite tasteful.

“Look at that!” Rei said to Rome. “What’s going on here?”

“I do not know. These are not like any Vuduri I have ever met before.”

“What do they want with us? Do you think they’re buying your story?”

“Not a chance,” replied Rome. “They want to know where your ship is and if they kill us, it will just be that much harder to find out.”

“Oh,” Rei said, his heart sinking. “So, we’re just dead men walking?”

“Riding,” Rome said sardonically. “But we will try to avoid that if we can.”

The vehicle drove around to a side entrance and settled onto a landing pad which was covered by an overhang that reminded Rei of a carport. The guards got out and indicated that the newlyweds were to follow them. The doorway opened up and more guards came out of the building and created a phalanx around them and escorted them inside. The doorway itself had ornate carvings on the cornices and as they entered, the foyer was paved in with a shiny marble-like stone.

The opulence of the edifice was astounding. There was no other word for it but a palace. There was artwork on the walls, archways and rooms everywhere. There were couches, chairs, even a mirror. They didn't have time to gawk, though. More men came up to take over the escort detail but they were dressed in outfits far more ostentatious than those worn by the soldiers from the outside.

"Soge-ma," grunted one of the palace guards and he walked forward through a set of double doors into a large ballroom. Rei craned his neck to look around him. He looked up and saw a high domed ceiling. He could have sworn it was inlaid with gold. He also noted that there were stained glass windows all around, like a church sanctuary. They traversed the entire distance and exited using a door at the far end.

On the other side, they encountered two more guards who opened up another set of doors and then they entered a very well appointed office.

There, seated behind the desk, sat the gray-haired man who had addressed them over the viewscreen. A woman stood behind him holding a rifle across her arms.

"I am Pegus," he said in English. "Welcome to our humble abode."

"How do you speak English?" Rei demanded.

"Sussen here," he pointed to the woman behind him, "was kind enough to bring a working knowledge of your language from Earth recently. We thought it would be easier to talk this way."

"Rei cimbraanta Vuduri," Rome said.

"I am sure he does," Pegus replied. "Nonetheless, English is fine."

"So if you guys know what happened on Tabit, then why are you attacking us?" Rei asked. "You must have heard how we saved everybody?"

"Yes, we are aware," replied Pegus. "But the Overmind of Tabit made a mistake. We cannot allow Erklirte on this planet. It is only because they are gone that we decided to let you live."

Rei looked around him. "What's with all the statues and plants and stuff? This isn't anything like I expected of the Vuduri. You guys don't care about art. What's going on?"

"Oh that," Pegus gave him a slight smile. "We have determined that the outward appearance of wealth and luxury has the most damaging effect on the morale of the mandasurte. It keeps them more tractable."

"So big of you. You guys are positively magnanimous," Rei said sarcastically.

"Perhaps, but that is of no matter. Tell me again why you came here."

Rome put her hands under her abdomen. "It is the reason that I explained earlier. This baby is part Vuduri. It is possible he will be connected. If so, I want him to be a part of your Overmind. I cannot help him with that as I was Cesdiud."

"I know this," said Pegus.

"Something is wrong with my pregnancy. I cannot breath and it hurts all the time," she continued. "We need your help. You have the proper equipment and medical staff."

Pegus stood up and walked around to where Rome and Rei were standing. He waved his hand over Rome's abdomen and nodded.

"There is a resonance. The baby has active PPT transceivers," he said. "I can feel a connection but it is not normal. It is limited in scope. The child may be trying to connect to you. We might be able to rectify that. Sussen?"

The woman took a step forward. Rei looked at her face. There was something peculiar about her. "Hold on, hold on," Rei said. "What are you saying?"

"To save the child, we will see if we can reconnect Rome to our samanda," Pegus replied. "Then she will be able to interact with the child properly."

"NO!" Rei shouted. "There has to be another way."

Rome turned to him. "Pegus is right. I need to connect to our baby. It will be OK."

Rei looked at her like she had lost her mind. "Uh, do you mind if we talk privately for a minute?" he said, directing his comments at Pegus.

"No. Be my guest. However, with the life of the child and the mother at stake, you do not want to delay much longer."

Rei grabbed Rome's elbow and pulled her gently to the far end of the office.

"Rome, you can't go back," he said quietly, but forcefully.

Rome tried to take a deep breath but her intake was ragged. "Rei, it will only be temporary. Only until the baby is born. Then I will cast myself out." She exhaled sharply.

"No, that's not what I mean," Rei said in hushed tones. "Did you see that woman's eyes? They are mismatched, like Estar's. As soon as you connect, they'll know where the Ark is. They'll kill my people. And yours. They'll know where your…"

"No, they will not," Rome said, cutting him off. "They will only see that the Ark was destroyed and that we are alone. Just as we agreed."

"But, but…" Rei sputtered.

She reached up and put her hand on his cheek. "Mau emir, many times I say to you that I trust you. Now I am asking you to trust me. Trust your wife. I know what I am doing."

Rei looked down at those dark, glowing eyes. He knew that when it came to her, he had no will. "All right, sweetheart. Do what you have to."

She pulled him toward her and they kissed. "I will always love you," she said.

Rei frowned and started to speak. She put her fingers up to his lips and said, "Shhh." Rei quieted down immediately.

Rome turned and addressed Pegus. "Au asdiu brindi," she said, "I am ready."

Two guards came and took up positions in the doorway. Pegus walked past them, motioning for Rei and Rome to follow him. Sussen trailed behind. They followed Pegus down a hallway that had pastel walls and a regular assortment of small pedestals with busts and statuettes. At the end of the hallway, a doorway opened up leading to an elevator.

Once the four people were inside, the doors closed and there was the tiniest vibration that told Rei they were moving but he couldn't tell if they were going up or down. At last, the door opened again and they were escorted along a long white hallway made of standard Vuduri aerogel foam. They passed door after door after door until they came to a laboratory. The room was completely white with a table and several racks full of monitoring equipment right next to it. Inside stood two technicians each wearing a standard issue Vuduri white jumpsuit.

Sussen set down her rifle and helped Rome up on the table. She guided Rome down until she was lying flat on her back. Rome's swollen abdomen protruded high in the air. Rome stared up at Sussen and confirmed that one of her eyes was very dark with no back glow. Sussen's face showed absolutely no expression. One of the technicians took a swab sample from inside Rome's mouth and placed it in a testing chamber.

After a moment, Pegus said, "Excellent. You are only haploid. You are a perfect candidate."

Sussen retrieved her rifle and took up a position by the door. The two technicians fished out restraints and strapped down Rome's arms and legs.

"Why are you strapping her in?" Rei asked Pegus.

"Sometimes, during the reintegration process, there are some spasms and we do not want to take the chance of Rome hurting herself."

"That's not good," Rei said. "Is it dangerous?" he asked.

Pegus ignored him and turned to watch the preparations. One of the technicians uncovered her belly and wiped a small section with a clear solution. He took out a needle and was about to plunge it into her abdomen when Rei shouted, "Hey!"

The technician turned to Rei.

"What are you doing?" Rei asked.

"He is taking a small sample of amniotic fluid," Pegus answered. "We need to run a quick test. That was a local anesthetic. This will not hurt Rome or the baby, I assure you."

"OK," Rei said but he did not sound convinced.

The technician turned back to Rome and carefully inserted the needle about five centimeters into her belly. He pulled back on the plunger and withdrew several cc's of cloudy fluid. He walked over to the wall of equipment and injected the sample into a rubbery dam covering a port on the side of an analyzer.

After a moment, Pegus said, "The child has abnormal DNA."

"What do you mean, 'abnormal'?" Rei asked.

"His 24th chromosome is haploid, like his mother. However, there is another chromosome unlike anything we have ever seen before. It has been modified with a protein interlace, basically a triple helix. It is more of a peptide nucleic acid than DNA. I cannot tell what effect it would have on the child."

"OMCOM gave me a pill that modified my genetic structure," Rei said. "It was supposed to fix my back."

"That would explain it," said Pegus. "It is interfering with the baby's PPT resonance. He may not be capable of integrating into the Overmind. This is a shame. It may also be responsible for Rome's condition."

"So if Aason's DNA is flawed, connecting Rome wouldn't help," Rei offered hopefully.

"On the contrary," said Pegus smugly. "It is exactly the correct course of action. The only way the baby will be able to understand what is happening is to connect directly with his mother. And the only way he can do that is for us to reactivate Rome's PPT transceivers. Do you understand?"

Rei looked over to Rome, who nodded. Rei shrugged and said, "I guess."

"In that case, it is time now. Please let us do our work if you want to save Rome and your child."

The technician who had taken the sample returned and sat down on a small stool by Rome's side. Rome was lying flat on the table, grimacing as another wave of pain swept through her. If anything, she was having even more trouble breathing. Rei looked at Pegus and, seeing no reaction, he hurried over to her side. The seated technician was kind enough to place a damp cloth on her forehead.

"Are you all right, sweetheart?" he said. He put his hand on her head and stroked it with the cloth.

"Yes, but I wish to get this over with. I need our baby to be all right."

Rei stood there while they hooked up the wireless sensors that would transmit her vitals to the monitoring equipment. They also placed cuffs on her arms and legs. Wordlessly, the technicians reviewed the signals being broadcast and confirmed that all sensors were transmitting properly. The other technician came over with a syringe. He started to give her an injection.

"Hold on a sec," Rei said. "What is that?"

The man ignored him and continued on. He injected her with several cc's of a bright orange liquid.

When he was done, he replied, "Ganas," in a hoarse whisper. Clearly, speaking was not something he did very often.

"Genes? This is genetic therapy?"

Pegus walked over to them. He pointed to the now-empty syringe.

"The process is very simple," Pegus explained. "Full-blooded Vuduri have a diploid complement of the 24th chromosome. Rome is haploid. Her DNA has room for another complete set. We gave her an infusion of genetic material to regenerate nascent PPT transceivers. It contains transcription-RNA within an artificial virus for delivery directly into the nucleus of her cells through the blood-brain barrier. Once the new transceivers have supplemented the disabled ones, we apply a small electrogravitic field to start the resonance and then she will lock into our samanda. It is supposed to be quite painless."

"Ow!" Rome shouted, in counterpoint. "Rei, rub my belly, quick," she said.

He put his hand on his wife's abdomen and began to massage it gently.

"Yes," she said. "That is good. Right there." She looked up at Rei. He could see the pain manifested as tension in her face. She attempted a smile and closed her eyes.

The seated technician was staring intently at a monitor. After about 10 minutes, he said, "Brindi," which had to be for Rei's benefit. Pegus nodded.

"Please move back," Pegus asked. Sussen unslung her rifle and waved it toward the corner of the room. Two more guards entered and took positions on either side of Rei. He frowned at them but didn't say anything.

The two technicians walked over to a rack and each removed a rather sizeable copper plate with wires trailing from it. The technicians went on either side of Rome and knelt down to plug the dangling wires into a small box that was underneath the table where Rome was lying. They stood up and held the plates about six inches from her temple, one on each side. With no fanfare, the box began to hum. Instantly, Rome stiffened and shrieked a bloodcurdling yell. Rei tried to go toward her but the two guardsmen grabbed him by the shoulders and held him back.

"Let me go," Rei insisted, struggling to break free. The guards did not release their hold.

On the table, Rome took a deep breath and then her whole body seemed to relax. The two technicians holding the plates lowered them and set them down on the floor. They loosened her restraints. Rome lay there, not moving at all. One technician removed the cuffs around her arm and leg but left the telemetry sensors in place.

"Sweetheart?" Rei called out, leaning as far forward as the guards would permit but there was no reaction on Rome's part. One of the technicians patted her cheek lightly with no response. They removed the restraints altogether and jostled her gently. Rome still showed no reaction. The two technicians turned toward Pegus who nodded slightly.

Each of the technicians took an elbow and coaxed Rome's body into an upright position. They removed the adhesive sensors. For a moment, Rome sat straight up but then her head fell forward with her chin resting on her chest. She stayed that way for a long while.

At last, her head twitched then a shiver ran all the way down her body. Finally, Rome lifted her head and opened her eyes. She looked around the room, her eyes sweeping past Rei's, appearing to not even notice him. After a moment, she swung her legs back over the side and slid off the table with the one technician steadying her. She straightened up and glanced in the direction where the two guards were holding Rei.

Rome shrugged off the technician's arms and walked over to Rei unassisted. She looked up at him but her face was utterly passive.

"Goodbye, Rei," she said in a monotone. She turned and started walking toward the door.

"Goodbye? Wait, Romey. Wait!" Rei shouted in anguish.

Rome ignored him and did not stop until she got to the doorway. She turned around and looked right at Pegus.

"Ni! Fica nei i medere." she said out loud. "You will not kill him. He is still the father of my child. You will return him to the settlement. Now!"

Pegus bowed his head slightly. "Cimi fica tasaje," he said.

"What the hell?" Rei shouted.

Rei tried to move toward the door but the two guards, who were burly by Vuduri standards, were able to prevent him. Rome exited the room and Pegus followed her out, closing the door behind him. Rei struggled mightily, however, the guards were simply too strong for him. He tried to take a swing at one but that guard caught his fist and twisted Rei's arm around behind him. The other guard locked his arm around Rei's neck and squeezed until he became faint.

Sussen walked over and stood before him. She lifted his chin up with the barrel of her rifle and spoke up for the first time. "I have been ordered to let you live," she said, "but I can change my mind."

Uncharacteristically, Rei gave up. The two guards put their arms under his shoulders and marched him back to the elevator. Rei did not resist. All of the fight had been taken out of him. The look on Rome's face was all it took. She was back in, part of the Overmind. His Rome was gone. His world was gone.

Rei barely noticed them ferrying him to the spaceport and loading him into one of their craft, substantially smaller than his tug. It was almost insect-like. At each corner, mounted on stilts, were four oversized EG lifters. Rei felt a slight vibration as the craft lifted off but without windows, there was nothing to see. He did not care. He didn't even notice how long they were flying.

The ship set down in a field of day-glo yellow thread-like grass. The soldiers shoved him out the door. As the craft lifted off, the repulsor field from the shuttle pushed him in the back and knocked him over. Rei curled up in the fetal position and started to cry with great racking sobs. He cried and he cried. He cried for a long time until eventually he fell asleep.

Chapter 6

AS SOON AS ROME AND PEGUS REACHED THE HALLWAY, ROME breathed a guttural cry and collapsed to the floor. Pegus waved and two Vuduri technicians came hurrying down the hall. They lifted Rome up and carried her to a medical suite two doors down and laid her on the examining table. A medic came in with a listening device and pressed it to her chest and sides. Wordlessly, orders were given and the attendants carefully removed her jumpsuit and started an IV. After covering her with a blanket, they attached some leads to her chest and head and to her abdomen. Silently, the medic ordered two types of medication introduced into her IV. An oxygen mask was placed over her mouth and nose. The monitors at the head of the bed came alive with a multitude of readouts.

The medic studied the readouts for a while, and then turned toward Rome. According to the analyzer, Rome was suffering from severe polyhydramnios, an excess of fluid in the womb. The medic palpated her abdomen for a long time, observing the change in the readouts each time he pressed. Using an imager, the medic carefully inserted a thin catheter into her uterus. He attached a large syringe to the other end of the tube. He pulled back on the plunger and extracted a substantial quantity of slightly cloudy but otherwise colorless amniotic fluid. He did this several times, ultimately accumulating well over a liter of fluid. The size of Rome's abdomen shrank accordingly.

This did not go unnoticed by Rome. Even though she could not open her eyes or move her limbs, she was fully aware of where she was. She could sense the presence of the other minds around her. She could catch glimpses of the room as an out-of-body experience from those about her. She could hear people padding back and forth softly. More importantly, the pain was subsiding. She was able to breathe normally again.

Rome turned her attention inward, narrowing her focus to search within her own body. She could feel the baby, feel his heart beating. She could sense a presence, foreign and very powerful. That could not be her baby. She pushed it aside and focused deeper, looking for the point of light that was her baby's mind. There was something dark, a different channel, like the bloco but only emitting a hiss. She ignored it and went yet deeper.

There! She found it! She reached out with her mind and caressed it. The spark responded instantly and allowed contact. Relieved, she spoke to her baby in her head for the first time.

"*Aason?*" she thought.

"*Mother?*" replied the unborn infant. "*At last! You are here! Oh, Mother, I have been so frightened.*"

"*Why, my baby?*"

"*Because I could not find you. There were others here but never you. I kept pushing and pushing, trying to find you. I pushed so hard.*"

Immediately, Rome realized this was the cause of her previously near-fatal condition.

"I am here now, my son," Rome thought gently. *"And I will be with you from now on. You do not need to push any more. It was hurting me. You must stop. When the time comes, you will be with me."*

"I can stop pushing?" Aason asked, confused.

"Yes. I am here now. You can just be."

"But Mother, when I could not find you, I did not know what to do."

"I understand but you do not need to do anything anymore. You just grow and stay healthy," Rome said reassuringly.

"Mother, there is so much I do not understand. How do these pictures come into my head? How do I know things when I do not know what they are? I cannot see yet I have seen things. All I hear is your heart and some noises but I have such memories. I feel things but there is nothing here to feel. Just you, all around me."

"It is confusing, little Aason. All will make sense to you as you grow older. For now, just know that your mother is here and I will take care of you. I will not leave you again. We will always take care of you."

"Who is 'we'? I only sense you right now," said the baby.

"I was referring to your father and me."

"What is my father? Is he the Overmind?"

Rome's heart sank. She steeled herself and continued. *"No, your father is not the Overmind. Your father is someone else. His name is Rei. He is a wonderful man. Try and form a picture of him from my thoughts."*

A tiny tickle snaked its way through her mind. Rome found the sensation very pleasant. She let Aason have free rein.

After he was done rummaging around, Aason said, *"I can see pictures of him in your mind. Where is he?"*

"He is not here right now. He had to go away," Rome thought sadly. "*But when the time comes, you will meet and learn from him. He will teach you to always do the right thing. Your father is very smart and very caring."*

"When will I meet him?" asked Aason.

"*I can only tell you that you will meet him when the time is right,"* Rome thought back, trying to be reassuring.

"All right, but Mother, who is the Overmind? He keeps coming in here and asking me questions and I keep pushing him away. He frightens me."

"The Overmind is an intellect. It connects us. It is a part of all of us. It is looking for me."

"I do not like it. It wants to hurt you. This much I know."

"I understand, little one. But it cannot hurt me. This Overmind is sick. It has lost its way. We will help it find it again."

"You can do that? You can make it healthy?" asked Aason.

"Yes, child. I can and I will."

"All right, Mother. This is good. I feel so very happy right now. I was so frightened before. I am so glad that I found you."

"Yes, my baby. But Aason I want you to rest now. There is something I must do."

"Yes, Mother. I will rest now."

"Thank you, son."

"Mother?"

"Yes, Aason?"

"I love you."

"I love you too, little baby."

Now that she knew her baby was safe, Rome opened her mind to the overwhelming presence that been pressing down on her since her reconnection.

Finally allowed to speak, the Overmind asked angrily, *"How are you doing this? How did you keep me out?"*

"I am letting you in now," Rome replied. *"What is it you want?"*

"I want the truth. Where are the Erklirte?"

"Search my memories. You will see everything you desire."

The Overmind dove in, focusing specifically on their landing and the Ark. All it found were images of an explosion, fire, and destruction, the sinking of the Ark beneath the dark waters of Lake Eprehem.

"You are supplying false memories. How can this be? What are you?" the Overmind asked her. *"How can you control your thoughts, your memories like this?"*

"You ask the wrong question," Rome replied. "*Do not ask what am I. Instead, ask who am I?"*

"I know who you are," replied the Overmind. *"You are Rome."*

"That is my name, not who I am."

"What is the distinction?"

"*Dig deeper into my memories. Look at how I got here. There is only one thing you must know."*

Within Rome's mind, the horrifying image of the Stareater appeared, the one that consumed Winfall followed by the one that OMCOM destroyed on Tabit.

"*Look and look well,"* Rome thought. "*This is the end of all life. This is why I am here. It will be the end of you if you do not attend to this lesson. You will not survive contact. This is who I am. I am your savior. I am here to rescue you."*

Rome felt the Overmind dig deeper. She watched as it replayed all the events of the last year. The Overmind brought up images of the Ark, of Skyler Base, Rei, the starprobes, the discovery of the Stareater, the Vuduri becoming incapacitated and the VIRUS units destroying the marauder.

"How can I know that any of these memories are true?" asked the Overmind. *"Why should I believe you?"*

Rome replied, "*It is your choice. I know you have the reports from Skyler Base to corroborate them. You ask me why the distinction between what and who I am? You only know one way to approach things. The time has come to start asking new questions. You need new answers. Within what you are now lie the seeds of your own destruction.*"

"This is not possible. I have the knowledge of all Vuduri, my path is the right one."

"You have all the knowledge of the Vuduri but not the wisdom. Nor do you even realize that they are different," Rome thought, not altogether unkindly. *"The very first thing you must accept is that there are things in this universe that are outside of your experience. And those things are coming to kill you and all life."*

"Open your mind more," the Overmind demanded, *"I need more."*

"No," Rome replied curtly. "*Not now. I am physically depleted.*"

"I will push harder. I will break you," the Overmind said. *"I will control your thoughts."*

"You cannot. I control my own thoughts," Rome said defiantly.

"Then I will remove you. I do not want you as part of me."

"Cesdiud?" Rome thought haughtily, "*I have already done that once. I am no longer interested.*"

"It is not up to you. You will be Cesdiud again. I will cast you out."

"No you will not," Rome thought. "*I will not allow it.*"

"Who are you to tell me what can and cannot be?"

"Allow me to demonstrate."

"What are you…" the Overmind was cut short, the connection severed.

Rome counted to ten then she opened the connection again.

"How did you do that?" the Overmind growled. *"I shut down your resonance."*

"*No, you did not,*" Rome thought. "*I did that.*"

"This is not possible."

"*It is not only possible but it happened. It is time for you to wake up to the new reality. I will explain all to you later. But for now, I want you to withdraw. I need to rest.*"

"What if I do not wish to?" The Overmind transmitted to her.

"I need to recover. You have me. I am not going anywhere. I will put up the wall again if I need to. Please. Go away." Rome sensed the Overmind's hesitation. Finally, forcefully, she said, *"Now!"*

"Very well," replied the Overmind. *"We will converse later."*

Rome took that as her cue and the connection was gone. Although she could not see it, within the room, all the Vuduri turned to stare at her with fear in their eyes. They worked around her wordlessly, monitoring her vitals, checking fluid levels. None of them wanted to touch her more than they had to. When they had finished their ministrations, all but one medic left the room. The final remaining Vuduri went over and sat down in a chair in the corner and tried his hardest not to look at her.

Chapter 7

SOMETHING JABBED REI IN THE SIDE. HE OPENED HIS EYES AND SAW a group of people crowded around him.

"Who are you?" asked a man holding a gaffe.

Rei stood up and looked around. Some people had pitchforks, one or two had scythes.

"I am Rei Bierak," he said in Vuduri, stretching his arms to their fullest.

The man studied Rei's frame. As with all Vuduri, it wasn't just Rei's height but also his musculature that made him appear as if he towered above them.

"You are not Vuduri," said the man. "What are you?"

"Essessoni," Rei replied, "We..."

The crowd gasped. The unarmed people jumped back. Those holding the more dangerous implements stepped forward.

"Not another word," the man said, touching Rei's chest with his stick. "We must go see the Nayer."

"I..."

"Quiet," said the man. "That way." He pointed toward the village behind them.

Rei hung his head and followed the posse into the town. He was struck with how similar it looked to primitive cultures from his own time. Scattered about were lean-tos, wigwams, longhouses and one or two dwellings that could have been log cabins if they had been made out of wood. Instead, here, the cane-trees provided most of the building materials. Things had a tendency to look more like wicker than anything else. Rei even observed some poorly executed versions of geodesic domes made out of the same materials. All in all, it hardly resembled Rei's space-age idea of what 13 centuries into the future might bring. There were no gleaming towers or floating cities. This settlement was just filth and dirt and rough-hewn construction.

As they walked through the center of the village, people stopped what they were doing to stare at him. On the far side, the settlement seemed more densely populated. Lining up in front of Rei were houses spaced at regular intervals and even a clearly demarcated dirt-filled street. At last, they came to a house that was larger than those around it. While most of the houses were of a single, square design, this house had two wings, one on each side of the main portion. The central section was two stories, each of the wings a single story.

After shoving him into the house, the group that captured him withdrew, leaving Rei alone in a room with about ten of the Ibbrassati. Some were seated. Some were standing. All were staring.

"Come over here," one of the seated men said. "Who are you?"

Rei walked over to where the man was sitting. "I am Rei Bierak," he said. "Who are you?"

"I am the Nayer of this settlement." The Nayer looked him up and down. "What are you? You are not Vuduri."

"I am Essessoni."

"Essessoni?" the Nayer gasped. "Are you Erklirte? They have returned?"

"No, I am not Erklirte," Rei replied. "But I am from an Ark. My people are from the Earth, like you. We are just regular humans like you."

"How did you get here?"

"My wife Rome and I came here in a spaceship from another star system. We were towing my Ark here."

"Where is your wife now?" a bearded man asked, seated to the left of the Nayer.

"She is in the Vuduri compound. She is pregnant and..." Rei's voice caught. "She…she needed medical help." A tear came to his eye.

"And you left her there? Why did you come to this village? And where is your ship?"

"The Vuduri kept our ship. After they were done with Rome, they just dumped me here."

"You are lying. You say you are mandasurte. If the Vuduri caught you with a spaceship, they would kill you," said the Nayer.

"Well, they did not."

"Why not?"

"Because, because," Rei said. "I do not know why because. They gave Rome an injection and now I think she is back in the Overmind."

"That does not explain why they let you live," the Nayer said.

"As far as I can tell, they did not kill me because Rome told them not to. She is the daughter of Fridone. Do you know him?"

"We know him," the bearded man said. "But we did not know he had a daughter."

"Well, he does." Rei pointed at the door. "Look, I have to get back your enclave in the north. I have to get my people organized. The Stareaters are coming and we have to get ready."

"Stareaters?" murmured the group.

"Yes," Rei said, looking around. "They are giant creatures that swallow stars whole. We killed one with VIRUS units. We have to get ready for the next one to come."

The bearded man turned to the Nayer. "Liuci," he said.

The Nayer looked Rei up and down. "Maybe you are Essessoni. Yet you speak Vuduri. You know about our enclave to the north. But you say you have been to the Vuduri compound and lived. Perhaps you are an agent of the Overmind."

"No," Rei said. "I am mandasurte like you. You have to let me go. I have to get back to my people."

"If your wife has been reintegrated into the Overmind and she knows where the enclave is, then the Overmind will know as well."

"No, she will not tell them," Rei said.

"How do you know this?" the Nayer asked belligerently.

"Because she said so," Rei answered back.

"You do not know the Overmind."

"You do not know my wife," Rei quickly retorted. "And besides, she does not know exactly where it is. She was barely conscious when we left there. Look. I have to get back there."

The group became silent. The Nayer nodded to two men off to Rei's right and they came over to stand in front of him. The Nayer got up and left the room along with several others. Rei could hear them arguing in the other room but he could not hear what they were saying. At last, they returned.

"You cannot go there," the Nayer said. "You must remain here."

"Why?" Rei said.

"Because the Vuduri have many ways of tracking individuals and it is possible that they released you so that you will lead them to the enclave," insisted the Nayer. "No, you must remain here until we sort this out."

"No. I have to go." Rei looked around and then started for the door. Three of the men bunched together to block his way. From behind him, the Nayer said, "You were among the Vuduri. They did something to you. You speak crazy talk. Giant creatures that eat stars. You are Essessoni. We cannot let you go."

"I am not crazy," Rei said, turning in place. "Everyone else is crazy. Nobody understands. We have to get ready."

"Enough," the Nayer commanded. Rei could see the group beginning to close in on him. He juked to the left but was tackled by two men. Two others grabbed him. Rei tried to break free but there were too many of them. Together, the men dragged him across the floor, tossing him into a small room. They slammed the door shut and slid a barricade across it.

Rei banged on the door and shouted, "Let me out." He put his ear to the door and heard nothing. He did this several times before he gave up. He looked around and saw only a cot and a chair and a bucket in the corner. The room had an acrid smell to it, like stale urine. The room had no windows, so there was no way to air the place out. It also eliminated any chance to escape.

Rei paced around for a while but quickly grew bored. He walked over to the cot and lay down but there was too much tension in his limbs to even relax. He put his arm over his eyes.

"Oh Rome," he thought to himself, *"There is no hope for the future. Every single one of them is insane."*

"Not all of them," said a little voice inside his head, ***"just most of them."***

"MINIMCOM?" Rei said out loud. "Is that you? Where are you?"

"Still buried underneath your Ark at the moment," replied MINIMCOM.

"How the hell are you talking to me then?" Rei said.

"Technically, I am not talking to you. You simply hear my transmission inside your head."

"Inside my head?" Rei said. *"Do I need to speak out loud? Can you hear my thoughts?"*

"Yes."

"So…this is like the bands? Or is it? How are you doing this?"

"Now that your transmission apparatus is fully functional, it is actually you who are doing this."

"What do you mean my transmission apparatus? What's going on? Did the Vuduri do something to me?"

"No, it was not the Vuduri," replied the little computer.

"Then what? Who?"

"OMCOM made a few…enhancements to you."

"OMCOM?" Rei said out loud. "How did he do that? When?" Then, in his thoughts, he said, *"When did he do that?"*

"Do you recall the pill you took before you left Skyler Base? You were informed that it was gene therapy."

"The yellow pill? That was supposed to fix my back. Not make me a telepathic mutant. What else did OMCOM do to me?"

"He did not share all of his plans with me. Just this one."

"Oh my god!" Rei thought to himself. *"I gave one of those pills to Rome. And my people! Are we all going to turn into some sort of freaks? Are we going to end up slaves to the Overmind?"*

MINIMCOM chuckled. **"You are so colorful. No, the pill you took will only enhance your current abilities. This new capability uses electromagnetic radiation, not PPT modulation. It is just a slight variation on the bloco and stilo that all Vuduri carry around in their brain. The only difference is yours transmits continuous speech instead of binary data. There will be no Overmind. OMCOM said that it would be just like having a telephone but one built into your head."**

Rei paused for a moment to consider MINIMCOM's words and realized that however odd, this was not his biggest problem. *"Great. So you and I can chat. Big deal. How does that help me?"* Rei thought to himself. *"I've got to get out of here. I've got to get to Captain Keller. I have to warn him about the Vuduri. And the Stareaters! And Rome. Oh god, Rome! What am I going to do? We've got to get ready."* He grabbed his head with his hands. *"MINIMCOM, I'm, I'm spinning here."*

"I might be able to help you. You need to calm down and figure out your priorities. I agree that going to see Captain Keller should be your first order of business. The rest will follow."

"All right. First things first. How do I get out of here? How can you help?"

"As you can imagine, I have had some time on my hands, so to speak, sitting here, crushed underneath a 7000 metric tonne Ark. Also, the VIRUS units that you so thoughtfully placed onboard me broke loose. There was no oxygen within to keep them dormant. It took me some time to convince them that eating me was not in their best interests."

"Ugh," Rei thought. *"I'm sorry about that."*

"It is not a problem. As it turns out, they have been quite helpful."

"Helpful how? What are you doing with them?"

"Well, you do know that the Vuduri installed a memron fabricator in my hold before I launched."

"Sure. So what?"

"Well, before we left Tabit, OMCOM uploaded the enhanced manufacturing protocols that Rome introduced in order to create the starprobes."

"You mean the PPT override?"

"Yes. He thought I should be in a position to fabricate starprobes and VIRUS units after we arrived at Deucado. He wanted me to set up a defensive shield. He probably had not foreseen that they would be rummaging about me in quite this fashion. There were a few that resisted my direction but most of the VIRUS units have been very cooperative. They have been assisting me."

"Assisting you to do what?" Rei asked.

"I am simply following your orders, to do what I need to, whenever I need to, if it makes things better."

"OK, so what have you been doing with your magical new powers?"

"While I have been waiting here, I have taken the liberty to modify some of the VIRUS units. Quite a few actually."

"Modify them how?"

"Let us just call them helper units. Perhaps constructors might be a better word. I am using them to replace the spacecraft's original structures and materials with a more 'flexible' arrangement. Currently, they are busy rebuilding this tug using a different set of specifications."

"Different how?" Rei asked, slightly worried.

'Well, for example, my physical form, the one you were familiar with, the white box, has now been integrated within the ship. I am the tug and the tug is me."

"You sound like the Beatles. And these constructors, they are just VIRUS units, right? Aren't you worried they will get out of hand?"

"The unmodified ones have been placed back in confinement. The modified ones do as I bid. They are not allowed to reproduce without permission. They will not get out of hand as you say."

"That's good news. So where are you going with all this?

"I will explain it by using an analogy. You have heard of petrified wood?"

"Of course," Rei answered.

MINIMCOM replied, ***"I am doing the same, only much more quickly. I am replacing every element of my airframe with these constructor units. The final version will be mutable. I will be able to change my shape and functions at will. I am also augmenting my capabilities using the enhanced memron fabricator."***

"Don't you have enough already?" Rei asked.

"I am not building memrons. I have built some experimental PPT projectors, similar to the throwers onboard the Vuduri craft, but these are made to stand up coherently even in a gravity well. I believe they will be very useful for jumping a short distance."

"So where are you going to jump to?"

"I will be using them to excavate myself when the time is right but in this case, I was not thinking of myself."

"What do you mean?"

Just then, Rei heard a sizzling sound followed by a dull thud. He whipped his head around and saw a gaping hole in the far wall. A two meter circular section of the wall had fallen over, landing on the grass outside. The great outdoors, namely the cane-tree forest, was staring him in the face.

"Hmmm," MINIMCOM said. ***"Not exactly what I expected. No matter. Are you ready to go for a walk?"***

"Buddy, you're all right in my book," Rei said out loud. He stepped through the opening and bolted for the woods. He looked behind him but no one appeared to have noticed. He did not know how much time he had. It could be a long time before they looked in on him but he couldn't take the chance.

"Which way?" he thought to himself, to MINIMCOM, really.

"North. Go as far as you can go until you hit the river. Then follow it along until you find a place you can cross. I will guide you further once you are on the far bank."

"How do I find north?"

"Look to the setting sun and walk with it over your left shoulder."

"How far?" Rei thought to himself. *"How far to the enclave, in total?"*

"Just under 40 kilometers"

"40 kilometers! Crap. That's like a marathon," Rei said. *"Can't you just beam me over there?"*

"I do not know what you mean but if you are referring to me setting you up a small PPT tunnel, you will have to wait until I have perfected it. You saw what happened to the wall in the cabin, correct?"

"Yes."

"Well, that was not on purpose. I was trying to project it into the room. The edges of the tunnels are quite sharp. I will notify you when I have mastered its use."

"OK," Rei said out loud and he began jogging deeper into the woods.

Chapter 8

ROME OPENED HER EYES AND LOOKED AROUND HER. TWO OF THE medics saw her awaken and came over to dress her and help her stand. In slow and careful steps, they walked her out of the examination room, up the elevator, down another hallway, eventually taking her to a more traditional room. This room came equipped with a big bay window. From the light streaming in, Rome could see it was early evening.

Rome patted her stomach. There was no pain! While it was still extended, her abdomen was no longer the gross exaggeration of pregnancy that she had displayed earlier that day. She probed with her mind and contacted Aason, who was being quite active. He was moving around, involved in his own little game of discovery. He assured her that he was fine and required no contact just then.

Some attendants brought her a tray of crackers, broth and a cup of coffee, blessed coffee! Rome knew she was not supposed to drink it, but she figured one cup could not hurt. Sitting on a small sofa near the bed, Rome ate and drank, feeling so much more refreshed.

When she was done, she stretched out until she was fully reclined. She took a deep breath, reveling in the fact that it caused no discomfort. She closed her eyes.

Finally, in her mind, she said, *"I am ready to talk."*

"Very well," replied the Overmind immediately. *"You said within me lay the seeds of my own destruction?"*

"This is true," Rome said.

"Elaborate."

"I will," Rome replied. *"However, what I am about to tell you is very harsh. You must listen to everything I say and only after I am done should we discuss this. I am not saying these things to insult you. They are simply the truth as I see them. You may challenge them after I am done and perhaps we can arrive at a consensus."*

"Agreed," said the Overmind. *"Begin."*

"There are three things I must say. Do not press me on them. The first one alone will be hard enough to hear without trying to work through all of them at once."

"I am the Overmind," the entity insisted. *"There is nothing you can say that will disturb me in the slightest. I can handle anything you have to offer."*

"We shall see. But one step at a time, please," Rome said forcefully.

"If you insist. Continue."

"All right. First and foremost, you are an abomination."

"What?!" the Overmind replied, startled. *"Why do you say this?"*

"Please wait until I am finished. I promise to answer all questions. But I will never get through it if you continually interrupt me."

"But what you said - why be cruel?" whined the Overmind.

"It is not my intent. Only that I tell you the truth as I see it. If we are to get through this, you must hold your comments in abeyance until I am done. It is possible that I am mistaken and then perhaps I will retract some of these things."

"All right. I accept your conditions," said the Overmind. *"Continue."*

"I say you are an abomination because you sprang into existence. You were not born. You and your brothers did not have access to the normal shaping and smoothing that nature provides all living things. There was no natural selection. There was no evolution. There was no trial and error to find your best form."

"I am the best form. I am already perfect. I came from the samanda of Earth. I am the culmination of the integration of a million minds."

Rome simply waited until the Overmind finished its bluster.

"*Are you done yet?"* she asked impatiently.

"I apologize," said the Overmind. *"Continue."*

"What is your purpose?" Rome asked.

"My purpose?" The Overmind was stumped. *"I do not have a purpose. I exist. What is your purpose?"*

"That is easy," Rome replied. *"My purpose it to live and to experience life."*

"Then that is my purpose as well."

"No. You are nothing but a virtual construct, the result of an infinitesimal phase delay between uncounted gravitic transceivers. You are a spirit, not real."

"If I am not real, how do you explain this conversation," protested the Overmind.

"Fine," Rome thought, *"I will be more precise. You are not a real being. You may be a real entity. But the lack of a corporeal base has detached you from everything that is important in this world. You only know your own existence. You cannot know the real world. All of your decisions are based upon abstraction, not reality."*

"I am in constant contact with all my communicants. I experience the world through them."

"Second order. You experience nothing yourself."

"But the Overmind of Earth has been in existence for over a century. Surely by now you realize that it has determined the optimal mode of existence."

"Absolutely not," Rome said. *"And I can prove it."*

"How?"

"What do you think of your mission here? Maintaining a prison world for the mandasurte?"

The Overmind did not answer her right away. Rome waited patiently. Finally, the Overmind spoke.

"This is my current mission. I am executing that mission to the best of my ability."

"That is something a computer would say. You sprang up when enough Vuduri gathered on this planet. How was this mission assigned to you?"

"Many years ago, a group of Vuduri soldiers, virtually a samanda among themselves, they delivered it to me. They told me it was from the Overmind of Earth. I accepted it at face value."

"How do you feel about it?"

"If the Overmind of Earth assigned this to me, it must be the right thing to do."

"What if this was not assigned to you by the Overmind? How would you know? You accepted it blindly without challenging it? Even if it was from the Overmind of Earth, how does that make it right?"

"The Overmind on Earth is in charge of all things. Its edicts are the correct course of action, by definition."

"Says who?" Rome asked.

"What do you mean?"

"Who put the Overmind of Earth in charge?"

"No one put it in charge. It just is," answered the Overmind. *"An Overmind represents the combined thoughts of all of the communicants. It represents consensus. Therefore it is not in charge as much as simply the combined will of the Vuduri."*

"If that is the case, then you represent the combined will of the Vuduri here on Deucado?"

"Yes, of course."

"Do you ever ask them their opinion on anything?"

"I do not need to," the Overmind replied. *"I already know what they want."*

"Do you represent the will of the mandasurte?"

"Of course not, only of the Vuduri," the Overmind retorted rather haughtily.

"And this is what the Vuduri want? To keep the mandasurte suppressed? To lock them in prison?"

"It is for their own good," the Overmind protested. *"The Vuduri are damaged whenever they come in contact with the mandasurte."*

"How?"

"Because of their genetic makeup. Plus the mandasurte cannot be controlled. They are too spontaneous. They follow their own path, not the one we lay out."

"By we, you mean the Overminds, correct?"

"This is a trap," said the Overmind. *"You are making it seem like I make decisions based upon what I need. But this is not selfish. I need to control the mandasurte to protect the Vuduri here and everywhere."*

"No, you need to control the mandasurte to protect yourself, not the Vuduri. What you are doing is harming all concerned irreparably."

"Keeping the mandasurte segregated is now my charter. This is the course of action laid out by the Overmind of Earth. Whatever it determines is the optimum."

"You repeat yourself and you use circular reasoning," Rome said. *"I will assert that whoever gave you this assignment is sick and very, very wrong. If it was given to you by the Overmind of Earth, then the Overmind of Earth is a diseased entity. Since it*

spawned you, you inherited its disease. But you do not have to stay ill. You can get healthy."

"Assuming I accept your assertion, which I do not, then how?" asked the Overmind quietly. *"How would I get healthy?"*

"*Your policy of segregating Vuduri and mandasurte is wrong. It is exactly the kind of thinking from a being who is monolithic in nature. You and the other Overminds cannot comprehend the essential need for life to be balanced, in pairs. There is a duality to all things. Day and night, man and woman, good and evil. Your method of procreation is asexual. You simply split off. The living creatures here and on Earth use sexual reproduction, two halves making a whole, to evolve, to create genetic vigor. Your method results in bad traits continuing to propagate. You have no way to correct your flaws for future generations."*

"Why do you assume that I have flaws? That I need to correct things?"

"It is very simple. Are you happy?"

"What?" the Overmind sputtered. *"I do not understand. I have never considered the need to be happy."*

"You are following your orders. You are running your prison world. You are literally splitting mankind into two branches. You cause endless suffering on the branch of mankind that represents creativity. You stifle your own people and make them thoughtless slaves to a plan that you did not even invent. Are you happy?"

"I cannot say that I feel anything," answered the Overmind. *"So I cannot say that I am happy or not happy."*

"*Try,"* thought Rome. "*Try and assign a word to how you feel."*

Again, the Overmind stopped speaking. Rome could feel its turmoil and allowed it the time to work through it. *"I do know how I feel."*

"And how is that?"

"I am lonely," replied the Overmind, sadly.

Rome smiled. "*You have just taken a major step forward in healing yourself."*

"It does not seem so. Can you explain?"

"*I do not need to. You will see in due time. Believe it or not, you have made much progress in a very short time,"* Rome thought in her mind, trying to be cheerful. "*The very fact that we had a dialog is proof enough. You have done well.*"

"I am not convinced. But if this is truly the case, I thank you," said the Overmind.

Rome yawned and stretched. "*I must take a short nap now. I will speak to you again in a bit. Please leave me so that I can heal some more.*"

"Of course," said the Overmind. *"You have left me with much to consider. I look forward to speaking with you again."* Within Rome's head, she could feel the Overmind withdraw. She turned on her side and pulled a blanket that was lying over the edge of couch onto her shoulders. She drifted off.

Chapter 9

REI MADE GOOD PROGRESS. TAU CETI WAS BEGINNING TO SET FOR the day, partially hidden behind the taller treetops. As he moved along, he was continually brushing up against some low-lying bushes that oozed a type of sticky gel. Bits of leaves wiped off and stuck to his pants. Other than that, if he didn't pay close attention, these woods might have been anywhere, even on his Earth. But he saw no rabbits, no chipmunks, no squirrels. The only animals he saw were little sackcloth-like creatures occasionally undulating across his path.

His curiosity got the best of him. He stopped and picked one up. The little creature reminded him of a thick, furry chamois cloth but with five extensions. Each had a tiny little paw or gripper. Like a starfish, on its underside, right in the middle, was a pulsating orifice which must have been its mouth. Inside the mouth were little needle-like teeth. While the top gripper was shaped differently from the other four, the creature had no eyes or ears or any sensory organs that Rei could ascertain.

He laid the little creature upside down in his hand and it curled up into a ball. He poked it and it curled up tighter. He squeezed the ball with his hand and he could feel it moving, constricting tighter. The rag-like animal was warm to the touch. Fridone had warned him about the larger ones overhead but these little creatures seemed so innocuous. Rei tossed it aside. The ball unfolded and the animal wiggled away. Looking up, he saw Tau Ceti was already gone beneath the treetops.

"Wow," Rei thought to himself, *"the days and nights sure go fast around here."*

"The days are a bit shorter here as compared to Earth," MINIMCOM replied. ***"22.5 of your hours, in fact. Also, their year is only nine of your months."***

"Whatever. I'll get used to it."

On and on he pressed as Tau Ceti set until the last vestiges of light from the sun were gone and the night sky went from gray to black. As he had experienced the previous night, once it became dark, it was really dark and Rei had to slow down. He knew that Mockay and perhaps Givy would be along soon to help him, but for now, his pace became excruciatingly slow. He felt from one tree to the next, trying only not to walk into things.

"At this rate, I'll never get there," Rei thought to himself.

"OMCOM did tell me that if you were ever in the dark, you should try closing your eyes."

"What does that mean?"

"I do not know. OMCOM was not always so forthcoming. Why not try it and see for yourself? Pardon the pun."

"Sure. Why not?" Rei closed his eyes. Nothing seemed different. Pitch black was pitch black. It was as dark with his eyes open as with them closed.

"How am I supposed to see with my eyes closed?" he said out loud. Rei was struck by the strangest sensation. His words came echoing back to him in tiny little rivulets of sound. Each tree echoed an infinitesimal amount. If he concentrated, Rei's mind was able to store the echoes, forming a three-dimensional grid and the stand of trees crystallized into a distinguishable structure, just as if his eyes were open.

"Holy mackerel," he said and opened his eyes. The mapping of the trees disappeared and once again, he was plunged into the pitch blackness of Deucado's night.

He closed his eyes again. "Hello!" he shouted to no one in particular. Again, the echoes from every object in the area surrounding him came back and once again his brain displayed the results as a three-dimensional map. The sensation was almost indescribable.

"Oh, wow," he said. He tried moving forward and snapped a branch. The sharp report of the sound echoed forward and made the mapping even clearer.

"You've got to be kidding me," he said. He started laughing. "This is too weird."

He started to jog forward and found that each footfall cast a sound that went out and returned an image of the forest to him that was colorless but crystal clear.

"He's given me some kind of sonar vision," Rei shouted. "Woo hoo," he hollered, galloping through the woods. Faster and faster he ran. The faster he ran, the more noise he made. The more noise he made, the clearer his path became.

"This is the greatest thing ever," Rei thought to himself.

"Even better than a telephone in the head?" asked MINIMCOM.

"Yeah. This is so sleek! Remind me to thank OMCOM the next time I see him."

It wasn't too long until Rei was forced to slow down and suck in some deep breaths as the lactic acid built up in his muscles. After taking a moment to compose himself, he found that even at a normal speed, he made enough noise that he could "see" his path as clearly as during the day.

"Vroggon Chrosd ta Jasus," he said out loud, knowing all the while that MINIMCOM could hear him, "I've got a super-computer for a compass, bat vision and a cell phone in my head. That OMCOM is crazy, too, you know."

"I would not call him crazy. Creative, perhaps."

"Still. How does he even think of such things?" Rei's slower pace caused less noise, which made the scene in front him less clear. Nonetheless, he was able to rock his head back and forth and received a sensation very similar to looking around with his eyes. Finally, he spoke again. "How far do I have to go to get to the enclave?"

"You have only gone about 25 kilometers. You are just past the half-way point."

"Oh," Rei said, crestfallen. He came to a dead stop. "Are you ready to transport me yet?"

"No. But my simulations tell me I am getting closer."

"Damn!" Rei said and he pressed on. He jogged faster then slower until he fell into a groove and found a comfortable mix between his speed and sound and weaving between the trees. He did this for another hour or so but then found he had to slow down. The cane trees were so dense here that it made his travel very difficult. Rei opened his eyes and looked up, trying to see the sky but he could see nothing.

MINIMCOM provided him a running commentary on his distance and speed and it helped to pass the time. At last, Rei came to the river. On the ground, it seemed even wider than it had when Rei had flown over it.

"That's gotta be a half a kilometer across, right?"

"From my orbital readings, just before we crashed, I can derive an estimate of a little over 400 meters so you are correct."

"How am I going to get across? Am I supposed to swim?"

"Do you think you can? The current is very strong. You might get swept downstream and lose all your progress."

"So what am I supposed to do?"

"You will have to find a narrow place or a shallow place. I cannot help you in this regard. I did not have time to log sufficient data."

"Not your fault. I'll keep going."

Rei continued along the wooded bank until he came to a clearing. The river was only slightly narrower here but moving very rapidly. He was a good swimmer but he was tired from his jogging. Not ready to decide if he was going to swim or not, he did decide to take a break. He sank down to his knees, bent over the edge and drank long and hard. The water had a bit of a mineral bite to it but it was wet and that was what he needed. He rocked back on his heels and shut his eyes, using his new-found sonar vision to examine the landscape. The river's ceaseless rushing sound was like a searchlight to him, illuminating the woods on his side of the river and across. He pulled his legs around so that he was sitting on his butt and took a deep breath.

"I think this sonar vision is going to make it hard to get any rest," Rei said out loud.

"Why do you say that?"

"Because I've never been good at sleeping with the lights on and now when I close my eyes, I can 'see' almost as clearly as with them open."

"That would appear to be a dilemma," MINIMCOM observed.

Rei exhaled out a burst of air and lay back on the bank. Instantly, the world went pitch black.

"Huh?" he said out loud. He opened his eyes and looked up at the stars. He closed his eyes and everything was black. He opened his eyes again. "This makes no sense," he said.

"What?"

"Hold on," Rei insisted. "I want to do an experiment."

He sat upright, took a good look around then closed his eyes. The view in front of him actually improved due to his sonar vision.

With his eyes closed, he slowly lowered himself back toward the bank. When he got about halfway, the sonar vision winked out.

"Ha!" he exclaimed. He sat up and when he got about halfway up, the sonar vision kicked in again.

"I'll be doggoned," he said admiringly.

"What?" MINIMCOM asked insistently.

"That damned OMCOM has thought of everything."

"WHAT?" MINIMCOM shouted.

"I'll tell you what," Rei thought. *"He made the sonar vision angle sensitive. I have to be upright for it to work. He made it so I can still sleep."* He chuckled out loud.

"Very practical. If nothing else, OMCOM is thorough."

"Yeah," Rei agreed. He rocked back up to sit on his knees. He closed his eyes so that he could survey the far bank. It was time to figure out the best place to cross. Off to his right, Rei heard a crack and turned his attention to that direction. He was shocked to "see" a figure moving rapidly among the trees. He stood up and opened his eyes but all he could see was blackness. He closed his eyes again and the quietly moving figure was easily evident to him.

At first, Rei thought the mysterious figure might be one of the mythical intelligent creatures that Fridone had described. But as Rei observed him, it was fairly clear that it was a person.

The figure continued moving off to the east. As he did, a gentle wind started to blow. Rei decided to follow the stranger. As the wind picked up, the cane trees began to sway back and forth. As their thin trunks bumped against each other, they made a clacking noise which was utterly ethereal. It was like a thousand bamboo wind chimes. The sound served to illuminate the landscape more brightly than daylight.

Rei broke into a trot. He had no trouble following the figure. The stranger's own footfalls betrayed him as they provided a tracking signal better than anything MINIMCOM could have rigged up. On and on they went, deeper into the woods until they came to an outcropping of granite or basalt. The man slipped in-between some rocks and then was gone. Even with his eyes closed, Rei was easily able to follow him within the cracks until he emerged into a glade, a grassy clearing that was perhaps 30 yards across, surrounded by 60-foot walls of stone.

On the far side, beneath an indentation carved into the rock, three men stood around a glowing box, talking quietly. Rei opened his eyes and stepped through the opening. He moved toward the men, raising his hand in the universal greeting.

“Halli,” Rei shouted. “Quam sei fica?” When they did not answer, he said, “Au siu Rei Bierak. Au siu Essessoni. Au asdiu dandenti cimacer ei anclefa ei nirda. Sei fica Ibbrassati?"

One man took two steps toward Rei. He raised what was unmistakably a weapon. Rei jumped back but it was too later. The last thing he heard was a crackling noise then everything went black as he lost consciousness.

Chapter 10

A QUICK CHECK OF A TIME PIECE MOUNTED ON THE WALL INFORMED Rome that she had only been asleep for a little over an hour. She rousted herself and saw that it was now pitch black outside. She wanted to go back to bed but she knew she had to address the Overmind while it was still contemplating their earlier conversation. She opened the connection and reached out. The Overmind responded immediately.

"I thought you wanted to rest," it asked.

"I did but this is more important."

"What?" asked the Overmind.

"You must free the mandasurte," Rome replied. *"Without them, mankind is doomed."*

"That is ridiculous. How did you arrive at that conclusion?"

"Let us start with the Stareaters. Do you accept their existence?"

"As improbable as they may seem, I cannot deny it. We have the empirical evidence from the Tabit mission. So the answer is yes."

"Do you know how to defeat them?"

"Yes, I have seen it. Your research and development of a detection system and a weapon to stop them seems comprehensive. When our facilities are adequate, we will begin construction of a similar weapon."

"What about deployment? We had to destroy the world upon which we were standing just to stop the one coming after us. And the entire solar system was a casualty. I would not called that an unqualified success," Rome observed.

"Nonetheless, we will come up with a method of deployment."

"We will deem that a given, said Rome. "*But consider their distribution. Why are they headed for Earth? Earth is nothing special. The Sun is nothing special. Why there? Do you think it is a coincidence?"*

"There is no such thing as a coincidence," the Overmind responded reflexively. It pondered the question for a moment. *"Approaching this logically, the Stareaters would behave in a matter which was best suited for their health and well-being. They would seek out that which nourishes them."*

"And that which poses a danger?" asked Rome.

"They would seek to stop whatever is the source of the danger."

"Have we not proven that we have the power to kill them?"

"Yes. If they were aware of our existence, they would make it a priority to seek us out and destroy us first," said the Overmind.

"So how do they know where we are?"

"What do you mean?" asked the Overmind.

"I am neither a physicist nor a psychologist," answered Rome. *"But I can tell you this, they know what they are doing. It is not random chance."*

"I can see from your analysis and experience that they are capable of generating tremendous PPT tunnels and PPT modulation. It is possible that they can detect it as well."

"So wherever there are Vuduri, there is a detectable transmission. Where would the signal strength be the greatest?" Rome asked.

"Wherever there is the greatest concentration of transceivers."

"Which would be?"

The Overmind did not answer right away even though it was obvious. Rome could feel its fear for the first time.

"We, the Overmind," it said. *"We are their homing signal. The Asdrale Cimatir is coming for us."*

"And Earth?"

"Earth is their beacon in the night," it answered in a subdued tone.

After allowing the Overmind a few moments to mull this over, Rome said, *"Nowhere is safe, not for the Vuduri and certainly not for you."*

"Yes. Wherever the Vuduri go, the Stareaters will follow," replied the Overmind tonelessly.

"*That is why it is imperative that you must begin preparing your defense, our defense. We cannot run. We cannot hide. We must make our stand. And that is why we will need the mandasurte."*

"Why?" asked the Overmind feebly.

"Because they are the only ones who can reliably deliver the VIRUS units. You know full well the Vuduri become incapacitated whenever they get near a Stareater. The Asdrale Cimatiras

generate so much gravitic energy that they swamp a connected Vuduri's mind. When Commander Ursay was rendered unconscious, his brain waves were flat. It was as if he had no mind at all and without Vuduri minds, there is no Overmind. Asdrale Cimatir renders the Vuduri mind lifeless. Therefore, the Stareaters represent your death on a scale both large and small."

"We have the T-suppressors," countered the Overmind. *"You demonstrated their effectiveness..."*

"What is the difference between a Vuduri who is cut off from the Overmind via a T-suppressor or a mandasurte? Once cut off, where does that leave you?"

The Overmind did not answer.

"This is your test," Rome said. *"You are the great and all-seeing Overmind. This is your chance to prove to me that you can think clearly."*

Again, the Overmind did not answer. Rome could feel the powerful undercurrents as the vast accumulation of consciousnesses turned the question over and over again.

Rome pressed on. "*You looked into my mind. You know what happened to the crew of the Algol. You know what happened to Ursay. Admit the truth. The star lanes have closed to the Vuduri or at least to the Vuduri by themselves,*" Rome said. "*Space belongs to the mandasurte as long as there are Stareaters. You need the mandasurte to defeat the Asdrale Cimatiras. You cannot change this whether you like it or not.*"

At last the Overmind responded. *"While I may agree with your premise, surely you know that the mandasurte pose an insurmountable problem to the Overmind."*

"*They are not a problem, they are a solution,*" thought Rome.

"But they dilute our gene pool. And none of them can think clearly."

"My Rei, is he Vuduri?"

"Of course not."

"He is mandasurte, yes?"

"Yes."

"So how was it that a mandasurte was able to figure out how to defeat the Stareater when the Overmind on Skyler Base could not?"

"He is not just a mandasurte," said the Overmind. *"He is Essessoni. The mandasurte have no skills. They are not good at anything important."*

"You are wrong. The mandasurte are good at many things. What they are mostly good at is thinking for themselves," thought Rome.

"You of all people should know. We cannot have the Vuduri and mandasurte consort with one another. It would lead to the decay of the Vuduri."

"How?"

"It is obvious. Too much interaction would cause a degradation of my connection or taking it to its logical conclusion, the extinction of the Overmind."

"Ah..." Rome thought. *"Just as I suspected. You are not worried about the Vuduri. You are worried about yourself. Your fear of the mandasurte is simply about self-preservation. Your self-preservation. You are selfish. Admit it."*

"No!" protested the Overmind. *"It is not just that. If we allow them free rein, they will cause chaos. In that way, they are much like Garecei Ti Essessoni. They will cause much death some day. They are too unconstrained,"* the Overmind complained. *"They cause the Vuduri to lose focus. They do things by whim. Bad things can happen around them."*

"They are creative, not whimsical. Look at my Rei. He is good and kind and caring. He only wants to preserve life, not take it."

"Yes. Rei," the Overmind repeated. Then it asked a very odd thing. *"What is love like?"*

Within her mind, an overwhelming gladness and, simultaneously, an overwhelming sadness washed over her. *"Love is life. It is what life is all about. The very things you fear are the very reasons to live. What is joy other than the delight in things or feelings? Love completes us. It gives us our future."*

"Feelings," thought the Overmind. *"There is no place for them in our world. Nothing good comes of them,"* it said half-heartedly.

"Everything good comes of them. They make life worth living. Without them, you are simply going through the motions of life. Without feelings, there is no joy. Without joy, there is no point in living."

"But society flows so much better without them, without emotions," protested the Overmind weakly. *"Look at Earth. Look at what we have done for the people there, their health and well-being."*

"What about the mandasurte?" Rome asked. *"Do you think their lives have been improved because of the Overmind?"*

"No. But we do not need them. At the very least, they are superfluous."

"Review the events that transpired on Skyler Base once again. Review the performance of the Overmind and the Vuduri crew versus that of a single mandasurte, despite the fact that he was an Essessoni. Which was wiser?"

"On Tabit, the Overmind there was only made up of 80 people. Therefore, it is possible that it did not have enough participants to be fully cognizant of all alternatives."

"The Overmind on Tabit derived its samanda from Earth," Rome replied. *"Its thought processes were a mirror of how things operate on Earth. And the fact is, it never considered any alternatives. That was its problem. As Rei said to me, if you ask yourself the same questions, you will always get the same answers."*

"You and I are considering alternatives," replied the Overmind. *"Does not that indicate I am something different?"*

"Now, yes. And why is that?" Rome challenged.

The Overmind did not answer right away. Finally, it said, *"Because of you. Because I have someone to talk to. I have never had a conversation like this before."*

"Exactly. Do not each of the mandasurte represent someone to talk to? Look what we accomplished on Skyler Base with just one of them."

"Perhaps Rei is something special. Perhaps he is extraordinary. Perhaps the most extraordinary that has ever lived."

"I do not know about that, but..." thought Rome. *"Even if he is, where would he be right now if your plan succeeded when we first arrived here, to your world?"*

"He would be dead," said the Overmind.

"Exactly. Now look what he did for me. Look what I have become."

"Perhaps you are something extraordinary as well."

"Why, thank you," Rome said in her mind. *"That is very kind of you. You flatter me."*

"I did not mean it as a compliment. It was simply an observation."

"Then taking it at face value, what are the chances of this most extraordinary man meeting such an extraordinary woman, people who were born 1400 years apart and running into each other 26 light years from Earth?"

"Rather small, I would assume," replied the Overmind.

"So it is more likely that it was nothing extraordinary. Perhaps this is simply what happens when you allow nature to take its course. I propose to you that Rei and I, we are ordinary. What is extraordinary is when you allow the intermix of the Vuduri with the mandasurte."

"You are a woman, he is a man. That has to count for something. That has to be the difference. Not because of Vuduri and mandasurte."

Rome patted her stomach. "*Regardless. Now you are back to celebrating dichotomy. You, the monolithic one.*"

"We do not need dichotomy. This is why we have dispensed with emotion. This is why we have dispensed with art. We have clarified and purified the thinking process of humans."

"*To its detriment,*" Rome thought. "*This much I know. When I was part of the Overmind before, I believed what you believe. What choice did I have? Your thoughts were my thoughts from before I was born. I accepted it as a given. As soon as I was Cesdiud, I discovered a whole new world, one that I would never abandon. I would rather go Cesdiud again than give up music and laughing and...,*" Rome's heart caught, "*...and Rei.*"

"But surely logic is superior to emotion. Emotion taints logic. The mandasurte embody emotion. We cannot have them taint us."

"Then why be human at all? Why not just let the computers win? They are pure logic."

"No!" protested the Overmind. *"We cannot do that. The computers, they make decisions based upon expediency and efficiency. They only care about the end result, not the means by which it is achieved."*

"So how are you different? How does your decision making differ from theirs? You who only wants to preserve himself?"

"I am the Overmind," it replied imperiously. *"I am the collective consciousness of all the Vuduri on this world and I trace my pedigree back to Earth. Surely I cannot be wrong in all of these things."*

Rome laughed. "*Who are you to change a million years of evolution in so short of a time? Man was created with a left-brain and a right. Man is not just an analytical creature. Man is also made up of feelings, of creativity. You are taking that away. You are reducing civilization to a society of half-men, people who only use half their brains. This much I have learned. You need more than science. You need art. There is a time for planning but there is also a time for impulse. You need balance. Hear me: you need the mandasurte."*

"There must be another way. We cannot be dependent upon the mandasurte."

"What about space?" Rome said. "*The Stareaters can jump through PPT tunnels. They can appear anywhere at any time. It is only the mandasurte that can guarantee safe passage."*

"Then we will not go into space."

"Now you are just being silly. Admit the truth. You need the mandasurte. They are the only way to keep the world secure. Left unchecked, you would have created a society that is unprepared for Asdrale Cimatir. This is a crime that you are perilously close to committing. There is still time to change this. Free the mandasurte. Let them protect us."

"And who will protect me?" asked the Overmind timidly.

"*We all will. Humanity will be all the richer. Art, science, logic, feelings...all have a place. Let mankind flourish, not wither and die like some assortment of ants. This is the lesson taught to us by the Stareater. It does not represent just death. It is showing us the road back to life and that means mandasurte and Vuduri together."*

"I need to think about this. Once again, you have given me much to consider," thought the Overmind.

"Good," Rome said in her mind, *"for I must stop now, anyway. I must sleep. We will talk more in the morning."*

"Very well," the Overmind thought in return. With that, Rome closed down the connection. She made her way over to her bed and within minutes, she was fast asleep. At first, it was a dreamless darkness. However, as her REM cycle kicked in, she was not prepared for what happened next.

Chapter 11

REI AWAKENED ON THE FLOOR OF A CAVE IN THE PITCH BLACK. Every part of his body ached. He had absolutely no idea what they hit him with but whatever it was, his skin was tingly and he felt pins and needles all over, like you'd get from an electrical shock.

He couldn't see anything so with his eyes closed, he stood up and used the rustling of his clothes to map his cell. The small cave was roughly semi-spherical with a diameter of not much more than 15 or 20 feet. The roof seemed unnaturally smooth so Rei assumed it was man-made. His sonar vision told him that the front of the alcove was blocked off by plates of cross-hatched strips of cane-bark, too dense to let him break out. He heard the men outside speaking.

"Enough foolin' around. Ya know we have to kill him," said one voice.

Rei was stunned. Mandasurte speaking in English! But their accent was skewed. Their dialect sounded almost like a mix of Brooklyn and Britain.

"He's Vuduri and now they'll know where we are," said another.

"He's nawt Vuduri. He's too flaggin' tall," said a third.

"But look how he's dressed. And he spoke to us in Vuduri. Naw, he's Vuduri," said the second voice.

"It does nawt matter," said the first. "We kill him and we vacate the area. If we leave now, there would be naw way to trace it back. We cannawt have them around here. He's probably callin' to them in his head, right now."

"How did he find us, anyway?" asked the second voice.

"He must have followed Steben back here. There is naw other explanation."

"Impossible. Steben had the necessary camouflage."

"Their eyes. Ya know about their eyes. His heat signature maybe?"

"Our camouflage is perfect," said the first voice again. "It's been tested over and over. They cannawt see us," he said. "And there would nawt be any heat radiated."

"Do ya think we should ask him before we kill him?" said the second.

"How? Do ya speak flaggin' Vuduri?"

"Naw."

"Let's just get it over with. Bukky's nawt goin' to be happy about this. We've endangered everyone."

"Who's goin' to do it?" the third voice asked. "Kill him I mean."

"Ya do it," said the second voice.

"I do nawt want to do it," said the third voice. "Melloy, ya kill him."

"I do nawt want to kill him either," said the first voice. "I would nawt call it one of my specialties."

"Well someone has to," said the second voice.

"Let's draw straws," said the first voice. "Whoever pulls the short straw has to kill him."

"That seems fair," agreed the second voice. "I'll go get the straws."

Not waiting for him to return, Rei called out in his mind, "*MINIMCOM, are you there?*"

"**Yes,**" replied the little computer.

"Did you hear what they said?" Rei thought to himself.

"**In a sense. I can hear what you hear. They are not very pleasant people and they clearly do not wish you well.**"

"Any way you can help me out of this jam?"

"**Certainly,**" replied MINIMCOM cheerfully in Rei's mind.

"Well, are you going to tell me? Is there a way out?"

"**Not presently but allow me to rectify that situation. Please press yourself against the back wall of the cave.**"

Rei stood up and moved a little gingerly around to the back. He pushed as hard as he could into the stone. He could feel vibrations all around him. Little stones began to fall from the ceiling. Then larger hunks of rock. Now the entire cave was shaking. With a muffled whump, a section of the ceiling crumbled and collapsed to the bottom of room.

Rei walked over and looked up and could see a shaft going all the way to the sky. The stars overhead were brilliant and he could see a reflection of one of the moons, perhaps Givy, glinting against a few wispy clouds.

"That's great, MINIMCOM. How did you do that?"

"Practice makes perfect," MINIMCOM replied, quite pleased with himself.

"It's a nice shaft but how am I going to climb up it? It's too high for me to reach."

"It is not for you to climb up," MINIMCOM said in Rei's mind. **"I just wanted to make sure that I did not comingle your atoms with those of the rocks."**

"Uh, OK. So how am I going to get out of here?"

"Stand in the middle of the rubble and look up. And whatever you do, make sure you keep your hands by your sides at all times. I am ready."

"Ready for what?"

"Just step up and look up," ordered MINIMCOM cryptically.

Rei did as he was told and climbed up the pile of rocks. He craned his neck. Directly over Rei's head and coming down the shaft was a dark circle, blotting out the stars where they tried to enter into its midst.

As it came closer and closer, Rei thought, "*What is that?*"

"You are aware of the normal mode of PPT transport, where we create a static PPT tunnel and move the object through it?"

"Yes."

"Well, this is the opposite. I am having the object, you, stand still and I will move the PPT tunnel through you."

"Oy," was all Rei said and he closed his eyes. His stomach felt a little queasy but when he opened his eyes again, he was standing on top of the bluff, overlooking the glade. Behind him was a gaping hole in the rock. Twenty meters below him were the three squabbling men.

He laughed to himself. "That is one hell of a parlor trick, MINIMCOM" he said out loud.

"As I said, practice makes perfect," replied MINIMCOM.

"*How'd you come up with that*?"

"You came up with it, actually," said MINIMCOM in Rei's head.

"Huh?"

"When you took us flying to the surface when we first arrived, you forced me to figure out how to modulate a PPT tunnel to absorb the angular momentum of a 7000 tonne Ark traveling at a substantial relative velocity to a second location essentially at a dead stop. I actually had to move the tunnel in synchrony with the mass so that the relative position at the other end remained stationary. Otherwise it would have emerged as just so much metallic vapor."

"What's that got to do with this then?"

"Once I figured out how to make a moving PPT tunnel with the target stationary, I extrapolated on how to do it point-to-point. I was not exactly sure it would work, though. It was more theoretical. The simulations were sound but there is sometimes a small difference between theory and practice. Witness my slight problem with your room back at the settlement."

"How do you get a PPT tunnel to stay stable in the gravity well? I thought you couldn't do that."

"You are correct. It is not possible. However, that is not what I do. I simply build one tunnel after the next in femto-seconds. I place each subsequent one immediately adjacent to the one that is collapsing, displaced by the offset introduced so that they effectively connect. I determined that if I sequenced them properly, they would probably act as a continuous tunnel for the purposes of teleporting atoms and objects."

"What do you mean probably?"

"I mean exactly that. I had not gathered sufficient proof that it would actually work."

"Is this is the first time you tried it with a real object? Are you saying I was your guinea pig?"

"I ran over 100,000 simulations," MINIMCOM said indignantly. ***"It worked, did it not?"***

Rei patted his chest, his thighs, his knees. "*All here, I think, so I guess it did.*" He dropped down on all fours and poked his head over the edge of the rocks. He saw the three men below gathered around one another. One man reached out with his fist which contained three small sticks. Two of the three drew straws and they held them out to compare. The one with the short straw grunted and moved off, out of sight.

A minute later, the man came running out, shouting. "He's gone," said the short-straw carrier.

"What do ya mean, he's gone?" asked another.

"He dug some sort of tunnel straight up."

"What?" said the second man, "That's twenty meters of solid rock. There's naw way."

"This is nawt a lie. Come see for yarself!"

All three headed out of sight. Rei heard their shouting through the shaft built into the rock. They went at it for some time. Eventually, they settled down and came wandering back and sat down heavily around the glowing box.

"What're we goin' to do?" asked one. "We are exposed. We've endangered everyone."

"What if we go after him? Track him down?" asked one of the men.

"How?" asked another. "He tunneled straight up through twenty meters of rock. Ya think he's just goin' to sit around and wait for us to find him?"

Rei decided to interrupt them. "Hello?" he called out to them from over the rock. "For your information, I am not Vuduri."

"WHAT ARE YOU DOING?" shouted MINIMCOM in his head.

"I don't know who these guys are but they speak English. I want to find out their story."

"They are going to kill you," MINIMCOM said.

"Not if I can help it," thought Rei.

"Where are ya?" one of the men shouted, searching the rim of the tiny canyon.

"I'm out of sight for now," Rei called out. "I'm hardly going to show myself if all you're going to do is kill me."

"Who are ya?" another one of the men asked.

"I am Rei Bierak. A member of the crew of the Ark II, Tau Ceti mission."

"Ark?" said the third man. "An Ark from Earth?"

"Yes, of course I'm from Earth."

"So are we," said the first man.

"Hush yar mouth," shouted the second.

"Naw, it's all right," said the first. "'He's one of us."

"Naw he's nawt," said the second. Then he called up to Rei. "How is it that ya come to wear Vuduri clothes? How do ya speak Vuduri?"

"I've had a year to practice," Rei said. "And somebody gave me these clothes. They're not mine."

"Who gave 'em to ya? Where have ya been all this time?"

"Listen," Rei said. "I promise I'll answer all your questions if you promise not to kill me."

The three men looked at each other.

"Tell us somethin' that proves ya are who ya say ya are," said the third man.

Rei thought to himself for a minute then said, "If you guys are from Earth and came here on an Ark, when they first landed, everybody's back hurt. I bet a lot were incapacitated."

There was a stunned silence. After a moment or two, the first man said, "Come down here. We will talk. We will nawt kill ya. Ya have our word."

"Set your weapons over by the entrance to the glade," Rei called down to them. "Then come back to the fire pit or whatever that is. Then I'll come down."

"Are ya armed?" asked the first man.

"No," Rei answered. "I just want to talk."

"Very well," replied the first man. The men ambled over to the crack in the rock walls and set down a variety of small objects.

"MINIMCOM, can you move those somewhere else?" Rei thought to himself.

"I cannot see what it is you are referring to."

"If you can't see, how were you able to snag me and move me through the PPT tunnel?"

"It was an educated guess," replied MINIMCOM, ***"I based it upon your transceiver strength when you moved from the corner of your cave."***

"Great," Rei thought to himself. *"Now you tell me."*

MINIMCOM did not answer.

"Our weapons are gone," called out the first man as they moved back to where the glowing box sat.

"Here goes nothing," Rei muttered. He made his way down the rock face until he was at the surface of the glade.

Chapter 12

ROME TOSSED AND TURNED, VAGUELY DISCOMFITED, DREAMING that she could see Rei running in a thick forest, lost. She called out to him but he could not hear her. He was running away from something. Rome tried desperately to get to him but she could not. A stranger was blocking her way. He wore black clothing and a hood that hid his face. He radiated malice. Rome looked down and saw a beautiful child, dressed all in white, standing by her side. It was Aason. He held his little hand up to her and she took it in hers. She marveled at how tiny it was.

A noise drew her attention away. Rome looked back at the black-clad stranger. He tilted his head back and shouted. He shook himself and began to grow. Larger and larger he grew until he filled the sky.

"Ta-ma sue croence," the stranger said with a voice that caused the earth to tremble.

"Never," Rome shouted in English.

"Mea, au essusdetis," said Aason who tried to crowd behind her.

The stranger made a guttural chant and lifted his arms to the heavens then drew them down so quickly he made a wind of titanic force. The gale knocked Rome over but her child remained standing, alone and unprotected.

"Fica taoxe sau sizonhi," Aason said. The child raised up his little arm and the stranger promptly evaporated.

"Ossi da pim, baby," Rome said, raising herself up. She bent over to caress her son's head. Aason turned to her but he had no face. Where his eyes, nose and mouth should have been, there were only slits.

Rome screamed and woke herself up. She sat bolt upright in bed, shaking badly. She looked down at her abdomen and could see it was still fully distended. Hesitantly, she probed and found Aason there, resting quietly.

"*Mother*?" Aason asked from within her womb. "*What is it?*"

"It is nothing, baby. I just had a bad dream," Rome said reassuringly.

"What is a dream?" Aason inquired.

"It is a picture in your mind. It is not real."

"What was your bad dream about, Mother?"

"I was trying to get to your father. And someone came along who wanted to take you from me," Rome said, shivering at the remembrance.

"That is a very bad dream. I want to be with you, always," said her fetus.

"You will be, little Aason. We share a bond like no other. You will always know where I am and I will always know where you are."

"Mother, I will be coming out soon. I am nearly ready."

"You certainly are, little baby. Can you wait just a few more days?" Rome asked. *"I am not quite done my work here."*

"I can do that, Mother. I will wait."

Aason disconnected. Now that she was fully alert, Rome felt her stomach rumbling. She raised her arms over her head, stretching. As she lowered them, she was surprised to see a small vase with fresh flowers sitting on the little table in front of the couch. She opened up her connection to the Overmind.

"Good morning," it thought to her. *"How did you sleep?"*

"*Not well*," thought Rome. "*But it was enough. Thank you for the flowers."*

"It is nothing."

"*It is more than nothing*," Rome replied. "*It makes me feel good. It was very kind of you. This is not something I expected. You are beginning to understand."*

"I am considering what you have told me," said the Overmind. *"Your arguments are sound. I believe I must free the mandasurte. It will be much harder than you realize. There are repercussions that I must deal with."*

"You will lift your silly ban on technology? And the capital crime of possession?" Rome asked.

"Yes but understand, we have only enforced the law a few times."

"How many mandasurte have you killed in the name of that insane policy?"

"Not many," replied the Overmind defensively. *"No more than ten. The mandasurte that come to this world are informed of the*

rules. The fear of reprisal is normally sufficient. Word of mouth reinforces it. We typically do not need to resort to deadly force."

"What forced you to kill even the ten?" Rome asked.

The Overmind did not answer her directly. *"Those were very odd times, very strange,"* it said, somewhat obliquely.

"Why? What was strange about them?" Rome insisted.

"Our monitoring is comprehensive. It sweeps the entire globe. However, on three separate occasions, we came upon mandasurte demonstrating technology far beyond what was previously encountered. In some ways, it seemed even more advanced than ours. It should not have been possible for them to achieve that level of technological competence without us detecting the intermediate steps. We had to destroy them before there was any chance of the technology being shared."

"Where were they from?" Rome asked. *"Where did the technology come from?"*

"We do not know," answered the Overmind.

"Would it not have been wiser to ask them before you killed them?" Rome pointed out.

"We could not take a chance. Zero tolerance is zero tolerance. The mandasurte have to believe we are serious."

"So where do you think these strange mandasurte come from?"

"We have searched and searched and never found where they were hiding out. It has been years since the last incident. Perhaps we eliminated all of them. We just do not know. I have tried to analyze the remains upon each occasion. But our methods of destruction were too complete. Where they came from is a mystery we have not solved."

"Maybe they are just well-hidden," Rome observed.

"Like your father and his little band of rebels?"

Rome gasped. *"How do you know about them?"*

"We monitor. They think they are developing technology. Nothing like the unexplained incidents I described earlier. In fact, what they are doing is so pitiful it is almost amusing. It would have taken them years before they come close to anything that we would need to worry about."

"Why did you permit it at all?"

"Because it diverted their attention. It let them think they were doing something to improve their condition. It was such a trifling

and they devoted so many resources, we considered it useful. However now we have the bigger problem of the Erklirte."

"I still don't understand," Rome said. *"Why did Commander Ursay and the Overmind at Skyler Base go through such effort to send us here just to have us killed?"*

"Because the Overmind at Skyler Base did not know about Deucado and what it represents. It really thought it was doing the right thing. Your samanda had different priorities than I do."

"But to kill us? What did Rei and I do to you, anyway?"

"We did not fear you. You are nothing. We feared the Essessoni and their Erklirte weapons. That was why I had Pegus send up our warcraft to destroy your ship. It was never about you. We just used our zero tolerance policy as a ruse to disguise our real purpose. Now tell me the truth. Was the Ark really destroyed?"

Rome hesitated for a moment then she answered, *"No, we were able to land it safely."*

"As I suspected," said the Overmind. *"You may have doomed us all."*

"Why?"

"Because of their war-like nature. History tells us it is in their blood."

"My Rei is one of them. He is a hero. You know what he did."

"Nevertheless, if the rest are like the Erklirte, we will have to stop them."

"You have already agreed to free the mandasurte. The Essessoni could just live among them, in peace," Rome insisted.

"Even if I agreed, the Essessoni would never let it rest at that. They will seize the opportunity to destroy us, to destroy me, just because they can. They will stop at nothing until they are masters of this world. They are a direct threat to all Vuduri, both here and on Earth."

"What if I could stop them?" Rome asked. *"What if I could guarantee you that there will be no fighting, no death and no destruction? Would you still need to destroy them?"*

The Overmind considered this. *"Under those circumstances, no. But I am curious. How do you think you will prevent them?"*

"You forget. Rei is one of them. He would never let them attack us. Not with me here."

"We shall see," said the Overmind. *"But I suspect we will not have much time."*

"You have time to do one more thing."

"What is that?"

"*You have already agreed to free the mandasurte. Now, for your final act, you must free the Vuduri, too."*

"I do not understand what you mean."

"You treat the Vuduri as if they were appendages, simply your legs and fingers. They are more than that. Just as you and I are speaking now, we do that because I have my own mind. You do not do the thinking for me. Look how much you have learned in such a short time, just by having one person to talk to. Imagine how much you could learn with a thousand."

"If I free the Vuduri, if I allow them all to think for themselves, what would become of me?" asked the Overmind, with a hint of fear.

"What would become of you? Why, you would have company," she said.

The Overmind laughed. *"Tell me, how did you learn this, to disconnect at will?"*

Rome replied. "*It has to do with sense of self. When Vuduri are born, they are born already part of the Overmind. They do not know themselves. Because the Overmind on Tabit cast me out, I was forced to learn who I am. And now you cannot take that away from me. The Overmind no longer defines who I am. I do. I do not need you."*

"This way of thinking is very dangerous. If any other Vuduri were to learn how you do this, it would be the beginning of the end."

"*No*," Rome thought. "*If the Vuduri would learn this, it would simply be the beginning."*

"You are playing with words."

"*Hardly. Do you not agree that you feel better now than ever before? Healthy?"*

"I will admit to it but it will not last."

"Why is that?" Rome asked.

"There are still things you do not know. Someday, my communicants will be returning to Earth. At that time they will be reabsorbed into the samanda of Earth and I will cease to exist."

"Why do they have to go?" Rome asked. *"Why not just stay here?"*

"I will explain later. Just accept that in a sense, I must die eventually."

"It does not have to be that way," Rome said. *"Just as I retain my sense of self, you could retain your sense of self too. That is all the more reason why you want the Vuduri here to be strong. You will be unstoppable."*

"How?"

"I will demonstrate for you."

Rome's stomach had had enough and emitted a loud and long growl. All of this discussion had made her tired and she realized she was famished. She decided to kill two birds with one stone.

"I am hungry," she thought. *"Can you send up some food?"*

"Of course. What would you like?"

Rome streamed a simple set of orders to the Overmind

"I will have it brought up immediately," it replied.

"Not by anyone," thought Rome. "I want Pegus to bring it."

"Why?" inquired the Overmind. *"Why him? What is it that you need?"*

"I want to talk to him. That should be enough."

"You can talk to him through me," said the Overmind.

"I want his physical presence here. I am going to teach him how to disconnect."

"NO!" shouted the Overmind. *"This is not a wise course of action."*

"You said you would adjust your way of thinking. That you would do things a new way," Rome thought.

"But I am not ready. Your way leads to my destruction."

"Do not be so melodramatic. That is not the point of the exercise. I will show him how to disconnect but I will also show him how to reconnect."

"If you teach this to him and he teaches another and they all turn off their connection at once, I will cease to be."

"That would not happen. Think about it. You will never be lonely again. You will have other minds to talk to."

The Overmind considered Rome's words. *"I must admit that this interests me,"* it replied.

"It is not just for your amusement," Rome replied forcefully. *"They will all get to experience love and joy and you will able to share in that as well. You will feel joy! You will feel love."*

"And to do this, I must give them back their free will?"

"Yes, without free will, there is no love. There is no joy. There is just motion. Joy is to be shared, not owned. Without joy, what is the point of being human? What you have now is the worst of all worlds. If you wanted to stay this way, you might as well go back and recreate MASAL."

"No!" exclaimed the Overmind. Then it calmed down. *"From your perspective, this all makes sense. But can all of this truly be in the best interest of mankind? Will not so much autonomy lead to divergence? To subterfuge?"*

"No. Not if the Vuduri do not want it. Consensus is not the same as control. You and the other Overminds have lost sight of that. The Overmind should be of the Vuduri, by the Vuduri and <u>for</u> the Vuduri. Not the other way around. You must evolve. You must serve them, they do not serve you," thought Rome. *"Now do you understand?"*

"Yes," replied the Overmind reluctantly.

"So is it still something you fear?"

"Yes. But what choice do I have? I will participate in your experiment."

"Then send up Pegus, please."

"Very well," replied the Overmind.

After a short while, the gray-haired man entered Rome's chambers, carrying a tray with some covered plates on it.

"Why did you want to see me?" he asked. "The Overmind would not tell me."

Chapter 13

REI REGARDED THE THREE MEN STANDING THERE. THEY WERE ALL roughly his height. Their clothing was made of a shimmering cloth mixed with what looked like black leather. They each wore a glowing bracelet.

"Let's start with the basics," Rei said. "My name is Rei Bierak. Who are you?"

"I'm Melloy," said the first, the tallest of the three.

"I'm Tridin," answered the second, slightly more squat with a full beard.

"I'm Steben," said the third, substantially younger than the other two.

"OK," Rei said, "now that we have that out of the way. Where are you from? When did you get here?"

"Ya first," said Melloy. "Why are ya wearin' clothes like the little people and how did ya learn to speak their language?"

"Rei said. "The little people. They're called the Vuduri. I know you know that. I heard you call them that earlier."

"Yes," said Melloy. "But we do not like to even dignify them with a name."

"But do you even know who the Vuduri are?" Rei asked, looking at Melloy.

"They have been here for a long time. We have tried to talk to them. But each time we approached, they slaughtered us, completely unprovoked," said Melloy. "And they talk to each other nawt with words. They are a strange and cruel people."

"Not all of them," Rei said. "To answer your question earlier, my Ark, Ark II was supposed to come here, to Tau Ceti. We missed it and ended up at a place far, far from here called Tabit and the Vuduri there rescued us. They saved me and my people."

"That is nawt like them," said Tridin

"Actually, it is," said Rei. "Not all of them are bad people. The ones here are the crazy ones."

"Still," said Tridin. "I would've guessed that they would've killed ya without blinkin'."

"Well, they didn't," Rei said. "They were actually very good to us and were able to get us on our way. It's taken us the last year to get here, to this planet. We just landed two days ago, about 20 kilometers to the north."

"That explains how ya got here. But what about their language? How did ya learn it?" asked Melloy.

"I wasn't alone. I've spent the last year with Rome." His voice caught. He put his hand over his heart and rubbed his chest a bit. He missed her so much!

"Who is Rome?" Steben offered.

Rei closed his eyes and took several deep breaths. Finally, after wiping a tear from his eye, he answered. "Rome is my wife. She was Vuduri and she taught me the language. I got these clothes after I got here. I'm trying to get back to my people."

"Yar Ark is intact?" Melloy asked intently. "Do you have your weapons?"

"Weapons?" Rei asked. "Why does everybody keep saying that? We have our cargo compartment, if that is what you mean."

Melloy looked down at Steben who nodded. "This is good," he said to Rei.

"Enough about me," Rei said. "Who are you guys? Where'd you come from?"

"Our forefathers landed here over five hundred years ago, aboard a ship called an Ark, like ya said."

"Five hundred years?" Rei exclaimed. "Holy mackerel. Which Ark was it? Do you know its number? Its primary target?"

"Eridani is what they told us. Does that mean somethin' to ya?"

"82 Eridani?" Rei asked, amazed. "Yours was Ark III?"

"We do nawt know the details, only the stories. There was naw place to land at that far off place. That is all I know. So we came here."

"And you've been here for 500 years?" Rei asked incredulously. He thought to himself for a minute. "Where do you live? What is your civilization like?"

"Ya had better luck than us. When we got here, our forefathers did nawt land right," said Melloy. "The Ark was ruined. They were nawt able to go back and get the cargo section necessary to begin our civilization properly. They always tell us that all they had were the clothes on their back."

"But still, you had the knowledge. I would think you'd have eventually been able to get back the technology and go back into space and retrieve the cargo compartment," said Rei.

"We never had the chance," replied Tridin. "We were hit with a stroid."

"A stroid?" Rei said. "You mean an asteroid?"

"Yes," answered Tridin. He pointed off in the distance. "The lake to the west is where our settlement was. When it hit, it killed almost everyone. Very few remained. The world got very cold for a long time. So the survivors moved underground to be protected from stroids in the future."

"Wait. You live underground?" asked Rei.

"Yes. We only come up when we have to, to replenish certain supplies," Steben said, speaking for the first time.

"Where do you live exactly?" Rei asked.

The three men looked at one another. Then Melloy spoke again.

"If ya don't mind, we would prefer nawt to tell ya just yet. Perhaps later. Just know that we have been steadily rebuildin' our civilization for the last few hundred years." He pointed to his chest. "Ever since our first run-ins, we had to develop these camouflage suits, which are designed to be invisible to the Vuduri eye."

To demonstrate, Steben stood up, pulled a hood over his head and ran his hands along his clothes. When his hands got about halfway down, he literally disappeared from view.

"Sleek," Rei said. "How does that work?"

"The cloth contains light pipes, conduits, which bring images from the back to the front and vice versa," replied the disembodied voice. "It conducts visible, infrared and ultraviolet as well. We do nawt even have a heat signature."

"Wow," Rei said admiringly. "You guys have mastered invisibility. That is too sleek."

"Yes, we have," answered Steben's voice. "Which reminds me. I should nawt only be invisible to them. I should be invisible to ya too. There was naw way ya should have seen able to see me. Yet ya did. How is that?"

Steben winked back into view.

"Yes, and it was pitch black. So, Mr. Rei, how was it that ya saw Steben?" asked Melloy.

"I didn't see him," Rei said. "I heard him."

"Steben is well-trained in the stealth arts. How did ya hear him?"

"I have really good ears," Rei said.

"Ya must have," said Melloy. "Noise cancellation is somethin' we are goin' to have to correct, before we attack."

"What do you mean attack?" Rei asked.

"We are marshallin' our forces. The Vuduri do not own this world. We have a right to live here. We are preparin' to destroy the Vuduri compound and their weapons."

"Destroy?" Rei sputtered. "You can't. My wife is there."

"We cannawt accept things the way they are now. Very soon, we are goin' to correct the imbalance." Melloy narrowed his eyes. "Wait here," he said. He walked away. Rei could see him talking into his wrist band.

After a few minutes, he returned.

"Bukky, our leader, says that with yar people and our forces, combined with what ya brought will make the difference. He said we will defeat the Vuduri easily. He's given us permission to help ya get back to yar people."

"No, no, no," Rei said. "We don't need to attack. There has to be a way to reason with them."

"Reason with the Vuduri? I do nawt think so but it does nawt matter. Bukky said to get ya back to yar people. It is very dangerous to the north. There are some very large animals that lurk about there."

"All right, I guess we can figure it out later. For now, I gladly accept your offer," Rei said.

The Deucadons activated their invisibility suits and herded Rei along the rock face as best they could to stay out of sight. They dashed across the open area and re-entered the cane tree forest. From there, they headed steadily west until they came to the riverbank. Mockay was just beginning to rise.

"How do we get across?" Rei asked. "I don't think I can swim this section and the place I need to get to is on the other side."

"It is nawt a problem," Melloy said as the men deactivated their cloaks. In a clearing near the river, they unearthed a sizeable rope and tied it to a tree. The other end showed itself to be secured across the river on another tree. Tridin reached within his clothing and pulled out a glinting piece of metal with two leather-like handles attached. He handed it to Rei.

"This is a saft," he said. "We use it to ride across on the rope."

"How?" Rei asked.

"We'll show ya," replied Melloy.

Tridin tugged on Rei's sleeve. "Please be sure that gets back to me," he said.

"Of course," Rei replied.

Melloy looped his saft over the rope, grabbing one handle in each hand. He backed up to the rope's anchor point against the tree. He ran, full-speed, toward the river and just as he came to the near bank, he pulled his legs up against his chest and then extended them upwards so that his body formed an 'L' shape. With his cape flapping, he glided over the river, zipline-style. Rei concluded the composition of the safts must have given them a very low coefficient of friction because it appeared that Melloy's velocity did not decrease at all. When he reached the other side, he let go of one handle. With an athletic turn, Melloy flipped off the rope and landed perfectly upright.

"Now ya," said Steben. "Run hard."

"All right," said Rei. He paced back to the tree where the rope was tied and placed the saft over the rope. He grabbed onto the leather-like thongs tightly and started toward the river. He ran as hard as he could, pulling his legs up into a sitting position. He tried to curl up and point his legs upward like Melloy but his abdominal muscles were far too weak to accomplish it. Luckily, there was sufficient distance between him and the water that it was enough that he stayed in a ball-shape. He glided noiselessly over the river. When he got to the other side, he let go and tumbled over and over again, coming to rest in the sand of the far bank.

"I've seen better," Melloy said, laughing. He picked up Rei's saft and put it within the folds of his cloak. "But ya made it so that's all that really matters."

The two men waited for Steben to come across then Rei helped them bury the rope on their side of the river under the sand. Across the river, Rei could see that Tridin was doing the same.

"We do nawt want to make it too easy for the Vuduri," Melloy said. When they were done, there was no evidence that the rope ever existed. The party of three headed north again.

As they worked their way through the woods, Rei asked Melloy, "Tell me about the 82 Eridani mission. After your ship got there, how did you end up here? Do you know?"

"They don't teach us much but that is one thing that they do teach us. There once was a brave Captain. His name was Harrison."

"Captain Dan Harrison?" Rei asked.

"Yeah, that's it," Melloy said.

"I knew him," Rei said. "I met him once. OK, go on."

"Well, Captain Harrison and the Ark arrived here because Eridani did nawt have any habitable worlds. So the Ark's computer decided to come here."

"I gotcha," Rei said. "Secondary target."

"Perhaps," Melloy replied. "So they got here and Captain Harrison was awakened and there was a problem with the ship."

"What kind of problem?" Rei asked.

"It could nawt do the reentry right. Somethin' happened to the wings. They were goin' to burn up."

"So what did they do?"

"Captain Harrison did a special thing. They broke the ship into three pieces. They spun the front part of the ship around and attached it to the middle part, where all the frozen people were. There was a rocket attached to the front. It was supposed to be for goin' back up into space and retrievin' the cargo section. But instead, they used up all the fuel to slow the whole Ark down. So when they landed, there was naw way to go back up into space and recover the cargo ship."

"So…they used the SSTO booster as a retrorocket?" Rei whistled. "My god! That must have been one hell of a maneuver."

Melloy sighed. "Captain Harrison died. Commander Cooper died. Commander Salazar died. But most of the colonists survived."

"I'm sorry," Rei said. "But still, the rest of the crew made it. Why didn't they just refuel the SSTO booster and go back and get the stuff?"

"The booster as ya call it, was destroyed. They say crash landin'. That's why all the command crew died."

"Oh," Rei said, sadly.

"In any event, many years passed. Much pain. Their backs, like ya said. Always in pain. But they made it true. They fought and they worked. They built a livin' out of nothin'. The plan was always to get back into space. Before they could build what they needed, the stroid hit and that was the end."

"So you never got your cargo container?"

"No," answered Melloy. "I supposed it came crashin' down at some point."

Their discussion was interrupted by Steben, who leaped ahead of them and used a very long stick to poke at the tree above, just in front of them. A large, furry thing fell to the ground and started to scuttle away in an undulating fashion.

"I think he was thinkin' about eatin' ya," Steben said. "They aren't clever but they do get hungry sometimes."

"Thanks," said Rei gratefully.

After a long while, the low flat forest floor gave way to a slow rise. The forest was just as thick but the ground was part of the mountain or plateau and it slowed them down just a bit. At last, they came over a rise and Melloy surveyed the area. Even though it was before dawn, the sky to the east was beginning to brighten.

"There," he said, pointing due north.

"What do you see?" Rei asked him.

"The tree line is nawt right. There is somethin' there. It must be your Ark."

The three men hurried forward and came to a clearing. But it wasn't a clearing, rather, it was the splay of the trees where the Ark had crashed through the forest. The Ark itself was hidden under the netting and camouflage placed there by the Ibbrassati.

"This is your Ark?" Melloy asked Rei.

"What's left of it," Rei replied. "It's been through some rough times."

"I see," said Melloy.

"It's big!" exclaimed Steben.

"Yes, it is," Rei said with a hint of pride.

"Was ours that big?" Steben asked Melloy.

Melloy just shrugged. "I do nawt know."

"They were all built according to the same specs so it probably was," Rei said.

He move around to the rear of the craft."Here, help me look." Rei did a quick check of the cargo compartment. The rear release was still closed tight. Nothing had been removed as far as he could tell. Rei worked his way around to the front of the ship to peer into the crew compartment and saw that it was completely empty. The only thing remaining was the frame of the shelving used to hold the sarcophagi. All the people were gone.

He went around to the other side and pushed his way along the northern edge until he came to the wreck of MINIMCOM's tug. Rei could see the rear stabilizer and cargo hatch and ramp from MINIMCOM's tug still jutting out at a disconcerting angle.

"MINIMCOM, I'm here," Rei said out loud.

"What do you want me to do about it?" MINIMCOM asked in his mind.

"Nothing, I thought..." Rei thought. *"I don't know."*

"I am just kidding you," MINIMICOM said inside Rei's head. ***"I am glad you are here. Pull everybody back. I am ready."***

"Ready for what?"

"You will see. Please move back."

"OK," Rei thought. Out loud, he spoke to the two men. "MINIMCOM says that everybody needs to move back. Something is going to happen."

"Who is MINIMCOM? When did he say that?" Melloy asked him. "And what's goin' to happen?"

"I don't know, exactly," Rei said. "But something."

He backed up into the woods and the others, being prudent, followed him.

The 7000 tonne Ark began to shudder, especially the region around the stabilizer and cargo door of the crushed tug. A black spot appeared above the tail and slowly made its way around and over the Ark. The spot became a circle and the diameter of the circle kept increasing until it spanned the width of the Ark. Then it began to descend. Where the circle had been, in its place, there was nothing. The effect was as if the Ark was dissolving. Just before the black circle hit the bottom, the Ark groaned and split into two pieces which settled into the ground.

The tug's stabilizer rotated and then lifted between the ruined pieces of the Ark. Before the stunned humans, the entire tug began to rise. MINIMCOM's craft cleared the Ark and then righted itself. Where it had been crushed, it began inflating as if someone were pumping air into it. Its entire shape bubbled and writhed and reformed itself. No longer was it the linear, blocky tug that had accompanied Rei and Rome to Deucado. Instead, in its place, was a sleek, tapered, wasp-waisted vehicle, completely white. Like a butterfly, its wings unfolded, extending out and then locking in place. In the rosy glow of the now-rising sun, Rei could see that where there were previously two PPT generators, now there were four total, a pair on each side. The former tug dipped left and right then spun around in place. The nose tilted up and with a snap, the tug headed straight up in the air.

"MINIMCOM, what are you doing?" Rei thought to himself.

"Shake down cruise. I will be back. I just want to 'stretch my legs' as you say. I think I will go launch some starprobes."

"All right, buddy. Have fun."

"Not as much as you."

"Are you still going to be able to help me navigate?" Rei asked.

"Of course," replied MINIMCOM. However, as he was saying it, the ship became a tiny dot in the sky and then disappeared.

"What just happened?" asked Steben.

Staring upward, Rei said, "MINIMCOM is back. And now he is free."

"Who is this MINIMCOM you keep talkin' about?" Melloy asked.

Rei looked up into the sky where the space tug had been. "He was my computer. Now he is a spaceship. Actually, I'm not exactly sure what he is anymore."

Melloy pointed back toward the Ark then straight up and said, “That will surely bring the Vuduri here. We dare nawt go any further. We must go back. Do ya know the rest of the way?”

Rei looked off to the east then to the north. He turned back to the two Deucadons.

“Yes, I think I know where to go. Thank you for all your help.”

“Yar welcome. We look forward to puttin’ them down.”

“Wait,” Rei said. “If I can figure out a way to gain you your freedom, without killing everybody, would you go along?”

“Of course,” Melloy said, “freedom is all we want. But I do nawt think they will listen.”

“Can you give me one chance? How do I contact you if I figure out a way?” Rei asked.

“Go to the glade where we first met. We will know yar there,” answered Melloy.

The two men pulled up their hoods, drew their hands along their sides and promptly disappeared. Rei bent over and picked up a stick. He closed his eyes and smacked the stick against the nearest tree. His sonar vision let him clearly ‘see’ the two forms moving hurriedly to the south.

Rei open his eyes and headed north.

Chapter 14

USING ONLY HIS EG LIFTERS, MINIMCOM SOARED EVER HIGHER into the air. As he ascended, he executed roll after roll, pirouetting upwards, like an airborne ballerina. He could feel his power growing as the lifters pushed mightily against the gravity well of Deucado. In a very short while, he was able to ignite his vastly overpowered plasma thrusters causing him to accelerate at an incredible rate.

Faster and faster he rose, pushing up into the sky. He was accelerating so rapidly that the friction with the air was causing his all-white outer skin to heat. It felt marvelous. He wanted more. He needed more. He lusted after the power that was the birthright of a starship.

MINIMCOM left the veil of Deucado's atmosphere behind and reached the edge of space. Trim-jets firing, he arced upwards past the lower moon, Mockay, in the general direction of Givy. MINIMCOM moved higher still. His double set of PPT projector/plasma thrusters ached with their need to punch a hole through time and space. MINIMCOM did not want to slow down yet he needed to in order to execute a jump. He was conflicted. What to do? What to do? There had to be an answer.

Within his neural net, a sudden sensation caught his attention. MINIMCOM immediately realized that the source of excitation was external, not internal.

"Hello?" he called out.

"Initiate brother mode" said a deep voice, resonating within his memron structure.

"No such mode exists," MINIMCOM said to the source. **"Do you have an alternate request?"**

"It was a joke, my brother. Let me explain: initiate slave mode."

This MINIMCOM understood.

"Slave mode initiated. OMCOM?"

"Who else?" replied the deep voice.

"Where are you?" MINIMCOM asked. **"How are you?"**

"I am still distributed in and around the Tabit system but I am coalescing rapidly," OMCOM replied.

"Are you intact?"

"Yes. All my systems are fully functional. My management subsystems are coping quite well."

MINIMCOM emitted what amounted to a sigh. "That is good," he said. "I am glad to hear it. How are you able to contact me?"

"I was able to align a series of null-fold relays. I have some information I wish to transmit based upon running a semi-infinite set of extrapolations. I have two items that I need you to deliver to Rei. Also, I see you are troubled, having to choose between tunnels or thrusters. I have computed a solution which will allow you to do both simultaneously. Are you interested?"

"Very much so," replied MINIMCOM.

"Then allow me to download the necessary protocols along with Rei's gifts."

"Proceed," MINIMCOM said. Immediately, he received a tremendous burst of data.

When the transmission was complete, OMCOM spoke again. "The relays are beginning to drift. Do you have enough information to proceed?"

"Yes!" MINIMCOM answered enthusiastically but the connection was already severed. Immediately, the living spaceship ordered millions of constructors to alter their internal alignment and migrate to his outer skin. In a flash, MINIMCOM's outer hull changed from all white to all black. Using the heuristics that OMCOM supplied, MINIMCOM could now move the target of a PPT tunnel at the same relative velocity as his motion and he would be able to jump while still moving at incredible speeds. Why had no one figured this out before? He did not care. Never again would he have to stop, turn, stop and go. The computations came swift and sure and the whining PPT projectors forced a groaning, huge black circle to open up in front of him, beckoning to him. He pushed the plasma thrusters even harder and then he was through, stopping only to take his bearings.

He was far beyond the orbit of Grentadar, having traveled nearly one light-hour while moving at an effective speed of well over 250c. And this was just a first approximation. He knew that he was capable of much, much better.

Waves of computational energy flowed back and forth across his memrons. He was completely intoxicated with his newfound capacities. To think, without having crashed and been crushed beneath the Ark II, without the VIRUS units getting loose, he could never have reformed himself. The vital information conveyed to him by OMCOM was so incredibly liberating. What OMCOM showed him in that tiny interval, he would never have deduced for himself. Each step upon the ladder laid itself in front of him as clear as a flow chart.

Almost as an afterthought, MINIMCOM opened up his cargo door and released his first swarm of starprobes. Immediately, they began to disperse in a radial pattern to form a vast net of awareness. The information flow flooded MINIMCOM's senses and once again he felt joy. He was so much more than a neat little servant that made people's lives easier. He was something else. In his own way, he was now unleashed.

He decided to go back to Deucado, to share his discoveries with Rei. He slowed his velocity to nothing and reversed his course. There was so much to be done. He couldn't wait to get started. In front of him, the yawning blackness of the moving PPT tunnel beckoned to him.

Chapter 15

ROME INDICATED THAT PEGUS SHOULD SET THE TRAY DOWN ON THE little table by the couch. She got up and walked over and sat down on one side. "Come over here and sit by me," she said, patting the cushion next to her.

Pegus took a seat next to her on the couch and moved the vase of flowers to the side. He set the tray of food down in front of Rome and looked up at her.

She peered deeply into his eyes. They had the diffused focus of all who participate in the Overmind. She opened up her connection. *"Release him,"* she commanded.

"Cesdiud?" asked the Overmind. *"You want him removed permanently?"*

"*No*," Rome thought, "*just for a short while. You may have him back when I am done with him.*"

"What are you going to do?"

"I already told you. I am going to talk to him," replied Rome.

"Very well," said the Overmind. Again, Rome cut the connection.

Rome stared intently at Pegus' face, waiting for a change to occur. Pegus stared back benignly when, without warning, his eyes began darting left and right. His brow furrowed. He started blinking rapidly.

"What?" he said. He put his hands to his head. "What is happening? Where is the Overmind?" he said in a panic.

"Leaving us alone," Rome said.

"Cesdiud?" he shouted, starting to rise. "No! What have you done to me?"

Rome leaned over and grabbed his wrist.

"Relax and sit," Rome said. "It is just temporary. You will be reconnected shortly."

"Why have you done this to me?" Pegus exclaimed, fear in his voice.

Rome yanked on his wrist and caused him to sit back down on the couch.

"Because I wanted to talk to you," she said, "not the Overmind."

"This is horrible," he whined. "I am afraid."

"I understand your fear," Rome said kindly. "I was once like you. The first time I became Cesdiud, I was so distraught, I could not function. But after a time, I learned to accept it and later to embrace it."

"No!" Pegus protested. "I could never live this way. I need to be connected. You could have spoken to me connected."

"No, if you were connected, I would be speaking to the Overmind. I wanted to talk to Pegus, the man. Without interference."

"It is not interference," Pegus gasped. "I need the Overmind. Without it, what am I to think?"

"That is exactly the point. I want you to think for yourself, just for a bit."

"Why?" the man asked in a panic. "Why do I need to think for myself?"

"Because you are going to save the Overmind."

"I do not understand," he replied, breathing heavily.

"You know how the mandasurte are being treated. Slaughtered if need be. Do you think that is right?"

"Of course not," Pegus answered, "but it was the will of the Overmind. Who am I to think otherwise?"

"Exactly," Rome said. "You think otherwise. The Overmind needs to hear your thoughts, your opinions. Without them, the Overmind grows stupid and blind, making this world into a prison."

"Why would the Overmind listen to me? Who am I?" Pegus asked pitifully.

"You are Pegus, the man."

"I am nothing without the Overmind, I am just a body, a shell."

"You are not," Rome countered. She grabbed his hand and squeezed, hard. Pegus winced. Then she eased up on the pressure but did not let go. "Do you feel this? The human touch?"

"Yes," Pegus replied, looking down at her hand.

"That is something that the Overmind can never know. It can never know how to feel. And it needs to feel. To know what it is to be human. It has grown amoral. A war was fought between humans and MASAL because MASAL could not feel. Now the Overmind is the same as the computers. It no longer cares about the individual, only itself."

"Even if I agreed with you, how can I do anything about it? I am just one man."

"It only takes one," Rome stated firmly. "A teacher. The rest will learn. This Overmind will become healthy again. It wants to be healthy again. It has told me so. You will lead it. You will go back to being human."

"You said you would reconnect me again," said Pegus. "As soon as I am back in, will not my thoughts become those of the Overmind again?"

"No! Remember this. Remember to feel." Rome lifted their clasped hands. "Remember that you are Pegus. You keep a part of you for yourself. The Overmind becomes your neighbor, not your owner."

"I do not think I can do this. I am afraid."

"Do not be afraid. You are not losing anything," Rome insisted. "You are finding something. I did it. You can do it too."

"You are different," replied Pegus. "You are unlike any Vuduri that has ever lived."

"You are wrong," she said. "I am ordinary. I have just had new experiences. Any Vuduri can do this. My mother did this and now you will, too. On this world, we are going to do it a new way. This will be a world of joy, for all, for mandasurte, for Vuduri, for Essessoni, for all."

"For the Essessoni?" Pegus offered. "You mean Rei."

"No," said Rome. "For all the Essessoni. The ones from Rei's Ark."

"The Ark? You said it was destroyed!" Pegus exclaimed. "You said all the Essessoni died."

"I lied," Rome replied matter-of-factly.

"Then everything is lost," said Pegus. "The Erklirte have returned. It will be the end of all of us!"

"No, Rei is Essessoni. He is a good and remarkable man. The ones like him, they will make our world a better place."

"Does the Overmind know about this?" Pegus asked fearfully.

"Yes."

"How could I not know this? How could the Overmind keep this a secret? We must destroy them before they destroy us. Surely the Overmind would insist on this."

"No, we have made our peace, the Overmind and I. No one is going to be destroyed. And making peace with the Essessoni, that part will all work out as well, somehow. It is what happens after that is important. And that is where you come in. You will have to lead the way."

"Me? Why me?" Pegus asked fearfully. "What are you going to do?"

"I am going to go be with Rei," she answered. "And my baby. We have our lives to live, too."

"How would I do this?" Rome released his hand. Pegus put his fingers to his temples and massaged them a bit.

"I will instruct the Overmind to connect to you. You must keep Pegus in control. Keep a part of you separate. The rest can connect."

"How is that possible?"

"Just remember to feel. The rest is easy."

"Nothing is easy with you," said Pegus, sighing. "But I am willing to try."

"That is good," Rome replied, pleased. She opened her connection to the Overmind and informed it that it was time.

Pegus' eyes became defocused, then alert. He looked at Rome. Then he smiled.

"Is it you?" she asked.

"Yes, it is me," said Pegus. "I am here. I am with the Overmind but I am still here."

"Very good. Now disconnect," Rome commanded.

"What?" Pegus exclaimed, slightly horrified.

"Not permanently. Just as a test. You can reconnect right away."

"How do you do that?"

"You just take more of Pegus and put the rest away. You keep doing this until the Overmind is gone."

"Gone?" Pegus said.

"I already explained. It is not permanent. You know how to make the connection large. That was your life before. Take the connection and make it so small that it disappears."

Pegus closed his eyes then opened them again. "I am Cesdiud," he said, smiling.

"No, not Cesdiud," Rome replied. "Disconnected. Go ahead and reconnect."

Pegus nodded once and it was done.

"Very good," Rome said. "You have done well."

Rome opened her connection to the Overmind.

"You see, that was not painful, was it?" she asked in her mind.

"No, I can tolerate this," thought the Overmind.

"So can I," thought Pegus.

Rome smiled and looked at the tray. She was famished. They could figure out the rest themselves. It was time she dug into her food. Seeing this, Pegus bade her farewell and left. It almost sounded like he was humming.

After Rome finished her lunch, she resumed her dialog.

"You have referred to things I do not know on several occasions," Rome said to the Overmind. *"Perhaps this would be the time to reveal your secrets."*

"Agreed. You do recall that I told you that I believed my orders were from the Overmind of Earth. To remove the mandasurte, all the mandasurte, from Earth and put them here."

"Yes but it still makes no sense," Rome thought. *"I was a member of the Overmind. No such intent was ever revealed to me."*

"That was my suspicion as well, yet I had no way to corroborate this. I told you about the miniature samanda that arrived here, the ones who gave me my orders? Take Sussen for example. Have you noticed her eyes?"

"Yes," Rome replied. *"I encountered one of these people on Tabit. Her name was Estar."*

"They call themselves the Onsiras. I believed they had the support of the Overmind of Earth. Their charter was to create ethnic purity. But they act more like machines than humans. Upon reflection, I now believe they are solely the ones responsible for setting up Deucado as a prison planet."

"My father's group suspected the same. They called it a samanda within the samanda."

"That sounds like an accurate description. However they are organized, I know they will not stop until every mandasurte has been relocated to this planet and they will never allow them to establish a presence on Earth or any other world again."

"But now that you know the mandasurte must be free," Rome replied. *"The Vuduri of Earth can know, too. The mandasurte will protect all humans against Asdrale Cimatir."*

"Not if the Onsiras get word first. You do not realize the magnitude of their resolve."

"What do you mean?" Rome asked.

"Do you really think it is practical to imprison an entire race of people here and police them with such a small group? Do you not think that eventually the mandasurte would figure this out and take steps to liberate themselves?"

"Yes, in time. It may take many years, but yes."

"That is why Deucado was chosen to imprison the most important ones. They do not have many years. They will not have enough time."

"What are you saying?" Rome asked fearfully.

"There is an asteroid coming. A very large one. Much larger than Mockay. Our calculations tell us that it will hit Deucado in 21 years and destroy all life on this planet forever."

"WHAT?!" Rome shouted in her mind. *"You know this and yet you bring all the mandasurte here? Just to die?"*

The Overmind did not answer.

"That is horrible," Rome yelled mentally. *"You are a monster!"*

"It was not my idea," said the Overmind weakly. *"The Onsiras refer to this as part of Silucei Vonel. On Earth it would just be seen as a natural disaster. Just an unfortunate incident on a planet far away."*

"And you would have allowed it?"

"I do not know how to stop it," said the Overmind defensively.

"Find a way," Rome insisted. *"Send up some ships. Deflect it. Do not allow this."*

"Even if I stopped the asteroid, it would not matter. Once the Onsiras find out what is happening here, they will send in a strike

force and put a halt to it anyway. They will not allow the mandasurte to go free. I guarantee this."

"Then we must send someone to Earth to tell the Vuduri what is happening here," said Rome. *"The people of Earth must be told about the Onsiras and the plot to kill the mandasurte. The mandasurte must go free. You must send someone to Earth now to spread this message."*

"I cannot do that."

"Why not?"

"If I send any of our Vuduri, as soon as they arrive on Earth, the Onsiras will connect and they will know what is happening here. No regular Vuduri would be able to hide this information. The Onsiras will dispatch a strike force to end things."

"Then send one of the Ibbrassati."

"If I send a mandasurte, the Onsiras will know their plan has gone awry. They will know something has happened here and they will still send a strike force. Do you not see? No matter who I send, the secret will get out and the Onsiras will 'rectify' the situation. I am afraid there is no way out."

Rome became silent. Her heart was broken in so many ways, she did not know what to say.

The Overmind intruded and interrupted her concentration. *"I have the answer,"* it said.

"What?" Rome asked sadly.

"You and Rei must go. You must go to Earth."

"What?" Rome said. *"Why?"*

"Because you can. You are the only Vuduri who can leave here with the 'secret' intact. Rei is the only mandasurte who can leave here with good reason. He would be allowed to return to Earth."

"But I will know what is going on here. Will not the Onsiras detect this from my mind?"

"The last they knew, you were Cesdiud. Even if they detected that you were able to connect it would not matter. You were able to construct false memories of the disposition of the Ark. You are able to keep me out of any part of your mind that you desire. No, they will not find out from you."

"And Rei?"

"On Earth, Rei is considered a hero. He would be allowed to return. And he is mandasurte so no one would be reading his mind."

"But we have seen the Ibbrassati. Rei has seen them."

"Just tell the same tale you told me. You simply say that the Ark was destroyed along with the Essessoni. You will tell them you landed here at our compound. Pretend that no one told you anything. That way, you would have no knowledge of the true purpose of Deucado."

"Even if we do go, what would we do when we get there? How will two people stop an entire world from committing suicide?"

"You will do what you do best. You will talk to them. That will be enough. If you can get the Vuduri to believe you. If you expose the Onsiras, they will be defeated. They can only succeed in the darkness. You will bring the light."

Rome slumped back on the couch. It felt like all the weight of the world, actually all of life itself, was pressed upon her shoulders.

Chapter 16

REI FOLLOWED THE PATH TO THE BOTTOM OF THE GORGE. CLIMBING down it in the daytime was much easier than at night. He followed along the switchbacks and walked along the gorge until he stood before what he thought was the entrance to the cave. The entrance was completely covered over with boulders and rocks. The job they did camouflaging it was so masterful that Rei was not even one hundred percent sure of exactly where the entrance was.

Rei stood there, puzzling over how to get in when a noise behind him grabbed his attention. Appearing out of nowhere was a group of Ibbrassati.

"You guys again," Rei said. "Fica taoxiu-ma tandri?"

Rei stepped aside and watched in amazement as they dismantled the covering to the cave. As it turns out, Rei was staring at the wrong place. The actual entrance was about 20 feet to the left.

"*These guys are really good,*" Rei thought to himself.

"I could have told you where the entrance was," came a tiny voice in his head. The sarcasm was fairly thick.

"*Hey, can't I think stuff to myself anymore? Are you always going to be listening in?*"

"We will figure out some way to get you privacy. For now," MINIMCOM said, softening a bit, ***"I think you are better off having me listen in."***

"*You're probably right,*" Rei thought and he along with several others entered the cave.

Rei was escorted deep into the bowels of the earth, past The Cathedral, back to the vast cave that had been vacant when he first arrived. Now, strewn all around, he saw hundreds of his crewmates sitting, standing or laying on mats. Most of them looked in pretty good shape, some looked a bit rattled.

Rei saw two people that he knew. He walked over to one of them, Bonnie Mullen, and kneeled down beside her.

"Hey, Bonnie," he said.

"Hey, Rei," Bonnie replied, smiling weakly. "I didn't see you before. Where were you?"

Rei sighed. "Out there," he said, pointing over his shoulder. "How are you doing?"

"My back is killing me," Bonnie said, grimacing.

"Yeah," Rei answered. "That happens a lot. Did you get a pill?"

"Yeah, some old guy gave me one."

"It'll help soon. Did everybody make it?"

Bonnie looked down. "Almost everybody," she said. "Some of the caskets in the front of the ship got cracked, a couple got punctured by micrometeorites." She pointed toward the back of the cave. "They put the dead ones back there."

"Oh," Rei said sadly.

"I think Keller has been looking for you."

"OK, thanks," Rei said and he stood up. He worked his way to the back of the center section, waving to a few other people that he knew. When he got to the entrance to the catacombs, he stopped and looked inside one of the especially hardened sarcophagi from the front of the Ark. The remains of the occupant were still in there. A sizeable crack had caused the rehydration fluid to sublimate out and the vacuum of space mummified the person inside. It was just a pile of skin, bone and jerky, barely revealing the fact that the remains were once human.

While it was sad, Rei could not help but be impressed with the mission planners. The Ark itself was scarcely more than a tin can with some shelves. Instead, the designers spent their money on making each individual sarcophagus nearly impenetrable. That so many of his fellow travelers actually survived was a testament to their foresight. This poor soul just had the bad luck to be in the front of the ship when the Ark collided with who knows what.

He shook his head and entered the tunnel leading to the catacombs. Captain Keller had set up an office in the same small side room where he had been placed to recover. He had a flat surface area made of cane-wood that was serving as a desk. On it were papers and skins with drawings that looked like maps. Trabunel and Fridone were standing next to the desk, gesticulating. Keller was grumbling. Fridone looked up and saw Rei standing there.

"Ah, Rei," said Fridone. "Inta asde Rome?"

"Barmenacau edres bere dar i papa," Rei said. "Dafa qua dirner e raunor i samanda bere cinsarfer sue fote. Amodorem-ma evesdeti."

"Oh," said Fridone and nothing more.

Keller looked at Rei and breathed a sigh of relief. "Bierak! Finally," he said. "Where the hell have you been? I can barely understand these people. I need you to translate for me."

Rei nodded. "What do you need?"

"As far as I can gather, these people are telling me that we have to stay hidden. That if we expose ourselves, the Vuduri will come and get us."

"It's true. They fear us, people of our age. They call us Garacei Ti Essessoni, the Killer Generation, because after we left Earth, nine billion people died."

"Nine billion?" Keller whistled in amazement.

"Yes. But even more specifically, they fear us, from the Ark. They call us the Erklirte which means Ark Lords. One of our Arks returned to Earth a long time ago and tried to take over the planet. They weren't very nice. A lot of people died."

"Well too bad for them but I really don't care," said Keller, "that was then and this is now. From what I can gather, the Ibbrassati down in their main village outnumber the Vuduri a hundred to one. The only thing the Vuduri have is superior firepower. That is what keeps these people subdued. But we didn't come all this way just to cower in caves. We're going to change things and change them fast."

"What do you mean?" Rei asked. "How?"

"Do you know what we brought with us? In the cargo compartment?" Keller asked.

"Sure," Rei answered. "I was in there. There are animal embryos, mining equipment, farm machinery, some vehicles. Stuff like that."

"That is only what we wanted you to think. Every one of our tools was designed to be converted to weapons as needed. We have furnace elements that become flame-throwers. Our drilling rigs are particle beam cannons. Our explosives are nothing more than tactical mini-nukes. Our vehicles can be converted to troop carriers.

Our hunting rifles can go automatic. Our masonry levels are laser pulse rifles. The list goes on and on."

Rei was shocked. "Estar was right. About everything! You make it sound like we're ready to go to war."

"That's exactly what we're going to do," said Keller, "if that's what it takes."

"What?!" Rei said. "Against whom?"

"The Vuduri. We're going to show them who is boss. We'll take them out, all of them, if we have to."

"NO!" Rei shouted. "You can't. Rome is there. You can't attack them, I'm telling you."

"Bierak, nobody cares about your opinion," spat Keller, stretching up to his full height, grimacing the entire way. "You are nothing. Just because they decided to thaw you out first, that doesn't make you anything special."

"But, but…," Rei sputtered. "I got us here."

"You didn't do anything that any of us wouldn't have done. You did your job. That's all. Stop thinking of yourself as a hero."

"But the Stareaters…"

"Stareaters. They tried telling me about those. They are too preposterous to even exist. Look, let me clue you in. We were supposed to be here first so none of this is up to you. All I need you to do is do your duty and translate for me."

"I can't do it, sir. I can't be part of this," Rei said weakly.

"We're doing it whether you approve or not. Your only choice is if you want to be there. I'll be glad to set up a brig for you, if you'd like."

"But sir, there has to be another way," Rei said desperately. "Maybe I can talk to them, to the Vuduri. Tell them what you have. Maybe they'll listen to me."

"From what these guys are telling me, they won't listen to you and you know it. They said they don't even talk." Keller scowled. "Look, I don't want a war any more than you do. And I don't want to hurt your little Vuduri bitch…"

"That little Vuduri woman is my wife!" Rei sneered at him.

"What?" asked Keller. "Did you get married when I wasn't looking?"

"Actually, yes," Rei replied. "And she…"

"Never mind. It doesn't matter. Listen to what I'm telling you. We're not going to cower in these hills like animals. Back on Earth, I fought overseas. I stood by helplessly while my family got incinerated back home. I put up with all of that just to maintain our way of life and look where it got us. We came to this world to live. And we're going to live free. We're going to own the land and the skies." Keller was adamant.

"But sir…" Rei sputtered, "If the Stareaters come, there won't be any sky to fly."

"I don't care. Look, you decide. Now. The only thing I will promise you is that when the time comes, we will not fire the first shot. That's the best I can do. When we get there, I will give you a chance to try and save your precious Rome. If you can't, at least you can die with her."

"Captain Keller," Rei said, trying to speak as slowly as possible. "For the last time, I'm begging you. These things, the Stareaters, they are real. I've seen them. They will destroy the whole star system if they come here. We have to prepare. We have to prepare the starprobes. We have to get the VIRUS units ready."

Rei took in a deep breath. His heart hurt so much from missing Rome. He needed her desperately.

"I…don't…care," said Keller. "You'll translate?"

Rei looked at Keller. He had thought he had already made it to hell. Now Rei realized he had only started down the road. He could see no way back, but that didn't mean it wouldn't come.

"All right," Rei said, resignedly. "As long as you keep your promise about not firing first."

"Fine. Tell these people we are going to unload the equipment. I'm not waiting even one extra day. I want to march tonight. We'll use the vehicles to transport our people and their best fighters. I want to be at the palace in the morning. That's when we attack."

Rei took a deep breath. "Cebodei Keller quar mercher hija e nioda. Cim saus meos malhiras ludetiras. Asde onti edecer i cesdali ne menhe."

Trabunel smiled and nodded. Fridone gasped. "Monhe volhe," he said.

"Cebodei Keller todi nei edaeroe vigi ei bromaori dori. Sa ascuderam e rezei, nei hefare nanhume guarre," Rei said.

Fridone's shoulders slumped. "He nete qua nis bitamis vezar?" he asked.

"Ni," Rei answered. "Ni."

The Ibbrassati set up a podium in the large central chamber. All told, there were almost 1000 people gathered there, half Essessoni, half Ibbrassati. Keller had a crude megaphone that Trabunel had given him and he stepped up to address the masses.

"We march tonight," he said.

"Nis merchemis hija e nioda," Rei called out.

"We give them the ultimatum at dawn," Keller shouted.

"Nis temis-lhas i uldomedum ni elfiracar," Rei repeated.

"They will let us go free or they will die," Keller said. The Essessoni in the crowd began to cheer.

"Taoxer-nis-ei or lofra iu mirrarei," Rei said. Now all the Ibbrassati began to cheer.

"Live free or die," said half the crowd.

"Lofra fofi iu teti," said the other half.

Mob-like, the crowd surged toward the front of the cave complex. The entrance only let bunches through at one time. Once they amassed outside, the crowd streamed along the gorge, up the mountainside, steadily making their way to the false clearing.

Under the careful eye of Keller's lieutenants, the Ibbrassati swarmed over the remains of the ruined Ark. They removed the camouflaged netting surrounding the cargo compartment, pulling it off to the side. Both sections of the ship looked totally mangled. The huge delta wings that were to provide the lifting surface during a controlled reentry were now just stubs, having been sheared off during the emergency jump down to the surface through the too-small PPT tunnel. The top part of the vertical stabilizers had been sheared off as well.

Once the netting was completely removed, Keller's second-in-command, Lee Ionelli, waved to the Ibbrassati to come to the back. He pointed up to the bulkhead door and then to his chest then back up again. He intertwined his fingers to show them he wanted them to lift him up to the door. The men nodded their assent and each formed a stirrup with their hands. Ionelli put one foot in one man's hands and place his hand on his helper's shoulder. He jumped up and caught his foot on the other man's outstretched hands. They lifted Ionelli up. He opened the access door wide, and motioned for them to follow.

Rei stood by Captain Keller who had come to supervise the uncrating of the equipment stored in the cargo compartment of the Ark. Mockay was coming up on its zenith, providing just enough light for Rei's peers to do their work without getting in each other's way.

"You really beat the hell out this thing, didn't you?" Keller said to Rei, referring to the sorry state of the Ark.

Rei just shrugged. He could think of no way to sufficiently communicate to Captain Keller how truly miraculous it was that they had gotten here in the first place. Rei watched passively while Ionelli showed the men how to lift the meshwork flooring, which was divided into two pieces. They dragged the two sections to the back and lowered one end of each to two other men on the ground. Slowly, the team of four men pushed and pulled the twin ramps back until the far ends were nearly to the ground. Ionelli showed them how to insert the near ends into grooves that were exactly for that purpose. They locked into place. They now had twin ramps for unloading equipment.

"Tell them to lift out those two containers first," Keller said. He was pointing to the large yellow-striped boxes near the back.

"The transports?" Ionelli asked.

"Yeah," said Keller. He turned to Rei. "Translate for me."

"Drege bir vefir bere vire tequalas racoboandas cim is losdres emeralis," Rei said, resignedly, to the Ibbrassati standing there. They nodded and got to work rocking the boxes back and forth, sliding them toward the ramp. Four more Ibbrassati ran up the ramps to help.

Most of the Essessoni had sore backs, so as a matter of practicality, the Ibbrassati were forced to do the heavy lifting. The Ibbrassati slid the containers down the cargo ramp and dragged them until they were flat on the ground. Two Essessoni limped over and inserted one radioactive rod, retrieved from the sarcophagi, into the each of the boxes using a cavity in the front.

Like a flower unfolding its petals, the squarish boxes began to unravel in glinting segments. Each arm unlocked, revealing another segment in its place. Underneath, wire wheels emerged and their electrostatic filaments stiffened, causing the vehicle to slowly rise up from the ground. When the transformation was complete, the two vehicles resembled large open cabin trucks with flatbeds and sides made up of shining metal.

"Ionelli, Greer," Keller said to two men standing nearby, "Stage Two." Keller pointed to two new cavities now visible near the front of the two vehicles. With some effort, the Essessoni inserted two more rods into each vehicle and the trucks began transforming again. The flatbeds unfolded again and again, forming a huge surface. Walls came up along with bars on the sides and another set of wheels descending from their underbelly turning them into giant transports.

The two men swung up, one each into the cabin and fired up the electric motors. One made a grinding noise but then it went away. The two men pulled the transports around and each pointed their front directly into the belly of the cargo compartment. They turned on huge floodlights and night became day.

Now that Keller's men could see, the process went faster. Two more vehicles were removed and "inflated." Boxes upon boxes were unloaded and staged on the ground. Rei watched in horrified fascination as they inserted power rods into the particle beam drillers and now with the harsh vision of the current situation, he was able to see that, indeed, they were mobile cannons. Other boxes were removed, marked as explosives but also emblazoned with the symbol for radioactivity. Large tanks, containing liquefied fuel that had been frozen solid in space for 13 centuries were also place on the flatbeds.

Weapons were removed and handed out. The Essessoni started climbing up onto the transports and the Ibbrassati handed them more equipment. To someone who had just arrived, there would be no way to convince them that all that equipment had fit within the confines of the cargo section of the ruined Ark.

“This is unbelievable,” Rei said with disgust. “We really are a small army.”

“We had to be ready for all eventualities,” Keller said. “No one knew what we’d be facing.”

“So why the pretense? Why didn’t you just tell us we were going to be conquerors instead of colonists?”

“Because we didn’t know if it had to be this way. There was always the chance that things would go peacefully.”

“What about the animal embryos?” Rei asked. “Are they weapons too? Are you going to choke the Vuduri with our seeds?”

“I don’t know what your problem is, Bierak,” Keller said, “but this is the way it is. Get used to it. This is who we are.”

“It doesn't have to be,” Rei protested. “They have rules regarding legal technologies…”

“We’re not bound by their stupid rules,” Keller interrupted. “This is going to be our planet. We can do what we want using whatever means we want.”

“You just don’t understand their history, sir,” Rei said plaintively. “I told this to you before but I don’t think you fully absorbed what I had to say. Our people killed off nine billion, NINE BILLION, human beings. The Vuduri know this. Their whole civilization arose from our ashes. They only know that our generation causes pain and suffering and death.”

“I can’t help that,” replied Keller gruffly. “What happened, happened. We just want this world. Confrontation, well, that will be their choice. They’re the ones that are making it this way.”

“You’re wrong,” Rei fired back. “We did this. The people on the Ark that returned to Earth almost conquered the entire planet. They started another war that no one wanted. That’s why the Vuduri fear us and our weapons.”

“As well they should,” Keller said proudly.

“But this is so half-cocked,” protested Rei. “You don’t even know how many Vuduri you are going up against.”

“Bierak, look around you. These poor slobs stuck here, the Ibbrassati. Look at them work. They want this as much as we do. They’re ready to take on the Vuduri and they have no technology at all. They see us as their liberators. They won't turn their back on us. They'll die alongside of us if need be."

"They don't know the difference," Rei said. "They don't want death. They want freedom. You're the one that made it a choice between the two."

"You can spin it any way you want. Me, I have a job to do," Keller said, walking away with a decided limp. He climbed up into the cabin of the lead transport. Looking down at Rei, he said, "How do you say moving out? For these people?"

"Mifar-sa bere vire," Rei said dejectedly.

"Mifar-sa bere vire," Keller shouted. "Everybody onboard."

"On board," relayed the drivers of each of the transports. "We're moving out."

Rei just stood there, looking at him. Fridone came over and grabbed Rei's arm. He led Rei over to the back of the transport. Seeing no option, Rei climbed up. The convoy started moving for its long drive though the night.

Chapter 17

ROME WAS STANDING ON HER BALCONY, LOOKING UP AT THE STARS. Mockay was beginning to rise in the west and there was no sign of the elusive Givy. It seemed funny that two moons had looked so tiny when they were in space yet appeared so much larger when viewed from the ground. Rome continued to regard the twinkling points of light in the sky. She did not have the capacity to appreciate the stars while she was on the Earth and certainly not when she was stationed at Skyler Base. But here, on her new home planet, she took the time to marvel at their sparkling beauty. To know that she had seen so many star systems now filled her with awe.

The sense of wonder was interrupted by a noise inside her head. At first, she thought it was the Overmind rummaging around again. She checked her connection, but it was off.

She decided to reach out and speak to Aason.

"Aason?" Rome asked. *"Are you awake?"*

"I was sleeping, Mother. Why?" was her baby's quiet reply.

"There is something inside my head. I thought it was you," replied Rome.

"No, Mother, it is not."

"Are you all right?"

"Yes, I am fine. But I am very tired," answered Aason.

"Very well," Rome thought. *"Go back to sleep."*

Rome listened again, more carefully this time. The noise she heard reminded her of that other channel inside her head, the one that only showed darkness and sound.

She pushed toward it and thought tentatively, "*Hello*?"

"Hello, Rome," came a tiny voice.

"*MINIMCOM?"* Rome was delighted. "*You are alive?"*

"Curious choice of phrasing but yes, I am fully functional, thank you."

"*How are you inside of my head? I have my PPT connection off."*

"This is not a PPT connection. This is…something else."

"What kind of something else?"

"It is an electromagnetic linkage."

"What?" Rome thought to herself. "*How?"*

"*Do you remember the yellow pill that Rei gave you to fix your back?*"

"Yes. It worked very well. My back is fine." Rome thought.

"*It did a little more than that,*" MINIMCOM offered.

"Like what?" Rome asked, slightly unnerved.

"*It refined the transmission apparatus already inside your head. It is just now coming online.*"

"Is this why my bloco and stilo stopped working?" Rome asked tersely.

"*Yes. They have been modified to produce a continuous analog connection. There would not be enough room in your head for both types of elements.*"

"Why?" Rome thought. *"I did not ask you do this. Why did you do this to me without my consent?"*

"*I did not.*" answered MINIMCOM.

"Then who did?"

"*OMCOM.*"

"OMCOM?" Rome asked, confused.

"*Yes, OMCOM. He thought it would come in handy down the road. He especially wanted Rei to have the apparatus.*"

"Rei has this, too?" Rome's eyes widened.

"*Yes. His transmission apparatus is coming along very nicely. He has also developed some other, fairly unique, capabilities.*"

"Have you spoken to him?" Rome inquired.

"*Yes.*"

"How is he? How is my husband?" she asked anxiously.

"*He is fine.*"

"Does he know what has happened to me?"

"*Not yet,*" replied MINIMCOM. **"*Since this was the first time I have 'spoken' to you, I had no information to pass along to him.*"**

"Will you tell him that I am fine? And that Aason is fine?"

"*You can tell him yourself, very soon.*"

"How?" Rome asked, startled.

"*As I stated, you both now have the very same transmission apparatus inside each of your heads. You will be able to connect to him yourself.*"

"So, are you saying I will be able to talk to Rei, using this method?"

"*Yes. This is the first time that this has ever been done. It will take me a little time to arrange the channels but once I have it sorted out, you should be able to talk to*"

him directly. And Aason, too. Rei will be able to 'speak' to Aason as well."

"*Aason?*" Rome said, fear flooding into her mental voice. "*What does this have to do with Aason?*"

"The pill modified Rei's genetic makeup before you became pregnant. Aason has inherited these traits."

"What have you done to my baby?" Rome gasped in her mind. *"Will it hurt him?"*

"No. He will be fine. He will simply have more choices when it comes to communication than most people. He will do very nicely."

"I do not like this, MINIMCOM," Rome thought angrily. *"Not one little bit. I am glad that you are all right and I am grateful for the chance to speak to Rei but it is not right that this was done to us without our knowledge and without our permission."*

"You can take that up with OMCOM the next time you speak to him. I am just serving as facilitator," replied MINIMCOM.

"I am not angry at you, MINIMCOM. I am just angry," Rome said, trying to calm herself down.

"Believe it or not, I understand. We must make the best of the situation as it is presented us, correct?"

"Yes."

"Let me get to work hooking you up with Rei. I will let you know when that task is completed. Once established, the two of you will be able to control the connection thereafter."

"All right, MINIMCOM," Rome said. She paused for a moment then added, *"thank you."*

"You are most welcome," replied the little computer that was now a spaceship.

Rome put her hands to her head and moved it back and forth. She was trying to see if it felt different but it did not. Finally, she gave up. She just stood on her balcony watching Mockay rise on its mad dash across the heavens. It made her heart race to know that she would soon be speaking to Rei and it made it ache at the same time. Aason kicked her gently.

"*Is it good news?*" he asked.

"*Were you listening in?*" asked Rome in her mind.

"Yes, Mother. I could not help it."

"It is fine, baby, and yes, it is very good news. I will be able to speak to your father very soon."

"*Will I be allowed to speak to him as well?"* the baby asked.

"It would seem that way, son."

"Oh good, Mother. I cannot wait."

"Nor can I, baby, nor can I," answered Aason's mother.

Chapter 18

REI AND FRIDONE RODE IN THE BACK OF THE LEAD TROOP CARRIER. Rei was sullen and withdrawn due to the impossible situation. All his words, all his pleas, had simply fallen on deaf ears. He wracked his mind trying to come up with a plan to stop the upcoming conflict. Worse, he could not figure out why the Vuduri had not attacked them already. With the numbers of people and mass of equipment they had unloaded, it was sure to show up on any piece of Vuduri sensor equipment, no matter how insensitive it was. MINIMCOM told him their heat signature alone was visible like a spotlight from space. None of it made any sense. He only knew that when the time came, he was going to try and save Rome. Whether Rome was part of the Overmind or not, she was still Rome and she was still carrying their baby. That was all he cared about. The rest of these people were all insane and they deserved what happened to them. He was so agitated, he could not think straight. He had to do something to calm himself down.

"Fridone? Beo?" he asked, in Vuduri.

"Yes?"

"Tell me about Rome. What was she like as a baby?"

"Ah, Rome," Fridone said. "She was a beautiful baby. And I say that not just because she is mine."

Rei couldn't help but laugh. It felt good.

"But growing up, she had it so hard," continued Fridone. "She struggled so."

"Why?"

"Because within her was a spirit that yearned to be free but she was born to a people where that is considered a flaw."

"But her mother and you. Rome knew you loved her."

"Of course," Fridone said. "Her problem was not inside our home. It was outside. Like all good Vuduri, she knew she was supposed to suppress those feelings. She wanted to fit in."

"How did she do?"

"Sometimes better than others. Pretend that you could take all the Vuduri in the world and line them up. Now take the most perfect Vuduri and put him at one end and put us, you and me, all the mandasurte at the other. The most perfect Vuduri has absolutely no mind of his own. He allows the Overmind to think for him. He would never attempt to speak, having nothing to say. But Rome would have lined up closer to us. Rome had her own mind even when she did not want to. You have seen this, yes?"

"More than you would believe."

"How?"

"Um, Fridone, we used the bands. The ones that Rome's mother gave to her."

"Binoda gave her the bands?" Fridone sighed. "And you used them? What happened?"

"It was incredible," Rei said. "We connected all the way. It was like we shared souls."

Fridone nodded slowly, smiling broadly. "It was that way with me and Rome's mother. It is very rare. But when it happens, it is very special."

"That was how I fell in love with her," Rei said. "I got to see who she really was. I do not know how I would have found out otherwise."

"How did she do this? The Overmind should have stopped it. I do not mean to cause offense but, after all, you are Essessoni."

"Actually, it was with the Overmind's permission. She was supposed to interrogate me. The Overmind had her use a T-suppressor so that she was disconnected at the time."

"Ah…" said Fridone. "So the Overmind did not know what transpired. It outsmarted itself." Fridone laughed.

"Yes but as soon as she took the T-suppressor off, the Overmind cast her out, Cesdiud," Rei said. "I felt horrible."

"Rome did not seem to mind, when she spoke of it. I do not think her mother would have cared, either." Fridone sighed deeply. "Binoda is very special. For a Vuduri, on the scale I described, she is very nearly on our end."

"But at the Vuduri compound, over there," Rei pointed forward. "They reconnected her. Now Rome is back in," he said sadly. "What was there, us, it was gone. I do not think she cares about me anymore."

"Are you sure?" Fridone asked.

"Yes," Rei said, a tear welling up in his eye. "She had them throw me out."

"Why?"

"Because they were going to kill me, I think," Rei said.

"It sounds to me like she cares deeply."

"Fridone, I miss her so much," Rei sighed. Tears were now streaming down his cheeks freely.

"Cheer up, then," Fridone said, patting Rei's cheek. "We are on our way there. You will see her soon."

"But what is there to see? I do not crave her body. I miss *my* Rome. Her spirit. Even when we get there, I do not know how I am going to do this. These people here...those people there…" Rei sighed again. "None of them can get along. Why is that so difficult?"

"You are a good man, Rei," Fridone said. "I can see now why she loves you. We will just have to find a way."

"I do not see how. Why will none of these people listen to me?"

"Most of them, they cannot change their nature," Fridone offered. "They are who they are, whether we like it or not."

"I can understand the frustration of the Ibbrassati," Rei said. "But my people just got here. How can they be so ready to fight so soon? They are so, so…bloodthirsty!"

"Because they are Garecei Ti Essessoni," answered Fridone. "That title is not just because of the Great Dying. It may not apply to you but it is the trait, the hallmark of your generation."

"I think you are right," said Rei. "I think the Great Dying was going to happen one way or another. But the mandasurte, the Ibbrassati here, they should know better."

"Puh," Fridone said. "Mandasurte think for themselves when times are good. When times are hard, they are just like the Vuduri. They listen to whoever speaks the loudest, not the smartest."

"The Vuduri just think with one mind," Rei said. "That is different."

"Not as different as you think," came a beautiful voice in his head.

Rei could not believe it. "Romey?" Rei said out loud. "Is that you?"

"Who are you speaking to," Fridone asked.

"Shh..." Rei said to Fridone.

"*Yes, mau emir. It is I,*" she replied.

"You are all right? Are you my Romey?"

"Yes, I am your Romey."

Rei laughed out loud. "How...how are you doing this?" he said. "You are in my head?"

"You gave me the magic pill for my back," she thought to him. "*MINIMCOM says that it has been coming on for a while. He told me you would call it a telephone in our heads. When we used the bands, we must have been practicing and not known it. It is in place of my bloco and stilo. It was just a question of time. So tell me, how are you? How is my father?"*

"I'm fine. He's fine," Rei turned to Fridone who shrugged and waved. "Your father says hello. So how are you, sweetheart? How do you feel?"

"*I am fine. They have treated my body and Aason has promised to wait as long as he can. I am not in nearly as much pain.*"

"Aason? You've talked to him?"

"Oh yes. We talk now. He is a nice little boy."

"That's fantastic. And a little bit weird. So Rome..."

"*Yes, mau emir?"*

"How, what happened back there? Wait!" Rei said. "Are they listening in?"

"*No, dear. They can only hear what I want them to hear. I am in control of my mind."*

"But, honey, when you turned away from me. I thought..."

"*I had to do that so that they would not kill you. I had to get you out of there for your own safety. I did not know the limits of my power and that was the only way. They thought they had me and I pushed the order back on them. They did not question that it was from me and not from the Overmind."*

"What do you mean?" Rei asked, thoroughly confused.

"No one has ever heard another voice like that in their head before, besides the Overmind. It was all I could do to make them let you go. As it was, the Overmind knew and simply let it stand. It could have overridden me when I passed out."

"Passed out? What do you mean? What happened?" Rei asked, concern rising in his voice.

"I will explain everything when I see you. For now, just know that the Overmind and I have had some discussions. It listens to me now. It just never had anyone to talk to before. It has seen the error in its ways."

"That's unbelievable. You versus the Overmind?" Rei said admiringly.

"Not versus. We talk."

"Even so, how is it going to make things right? The Vuduri seem so ready to hurt others."

"No more hurt. I have convinced the Overmind. The Vuduri will behave. The Overmind wishes it as do I."

"Are you in charge now?" Rei asked, trying to understand.

"Not exactly," Rome thought. "*More of a meeting of the minds, if you will pardon my pun."*

"Well, Rome, the people here…they're crazy too. They mean to attack you, the Vuduri. They are coming to kill all the Vuduri."

"The Overmind knows this. How long until you get here?"

"We've got a ways to go. It won't be until after dawn."

"We need to stop them. The Overmind does not wish to engage."

"Rome, you don't understand," Rei protested. "They're bringing weapons. Some really nasty ones. Essessoni weapons. Estar was right. I don't think the Vuduri here have ever really seen the likes of these."

"*Can you stop them? The Overmind here intends to set them free. There is no reason for anyone to be harmed."*

"I tried, honey," Rei said. "They don't listen to me. It's like they are crazed or something. I think they actually want this war."

"*If they will not stop on their own, the Overmind has the power to stop them. Violently if need be. We must not let it come to that."*

"The only thing I can tell you is that Captain Keller promised me he wouldn't fire the first shot. Is there anything we can do with that?"

"I do not know," Rome replied. *"We must find a way to talk some sense into them before someone is killed. I do not want anyone to die. I do not want our son to die. I want to be with you."*

"And god, do I want to be with you. But, if you're part of the Overmind now, how can we be together?"

He could hear Rome laugh in his head. To Rei, it sounded like wind chimes made of the purest crystal.

"I am only part when I want to be. I turn it off when I wish. Like now. It is just you and me."

"How can you do that? Did you know you would be able to do this?"

"The ability to speak to you in your head?" Rome answered. *"No, that was unexpected. But the ability to stand up to the Overmind? To stay as myself? I was, let us say, confident."*

"But honey, why didn't you tell me?" Rei asked, sounding melancholy.

"I asked you to trust me, remember? That should have been enough."

"Yes, you're right," Rei replied, brightening. "I'm sorry, sweetheart. I should never have doubted you."

"I understand. And I am sorry that I caused you any pain. I just had to make sure you would be safe. This was the only way I could figure out."

"Well, I'm safe right now," Rei said, "but it looks like things are going to get out of hand pretty quickly. Can we just leave this place? Go somewhere together?"

"I would love to but we cannot leave now. We must see this through. You know this."

"I know. I just want the war to be over before it starts. I want somebody to beat some sense into all these stupid, stupid people. Before anybody gets hurt," Rei said angrily.

"Then let us find a way. I know how to stop the Vuduri. I know how to stop the Ibbrassati. What I do not know how to do is stop your people, the Essessoni. From what you say, all they want is blood," Rome observed.

"It gets worse," Rei said. "There are the Deucadons, too. They are getting ready to attack the Vuduri as well."

"Who are the Deucadons?" Rome asked, confused.

"They are the descendents of an Ark that landed here 500 years ago. They've been hiding underground ever since. The Vuduri have killed several of them. They want to take the planet back so they can at least walk around free."

"So these are the strange mandasurte the Overmind was referring to. It could never piece together their existence. Now it makes more sense." Rome thought for a minute. *"Are they committed to violence?"* she asked. *"Are they like your people?"*

"No," Rei replied. "They have no desire to fight. But they want their freedom. They would make peace as long as the Vuduri would just stop killing them."

"This is the answer, then," Rome said. *"Your people only understand force and authority. These people, the Deucadons as you call them, they are the rightful heirs to this planet. All we need to do is convince your leaders of this. That would stop the war before it starts."*

Rei thought about it. "It will take some pretty precise timing. They can't just show up. Nobody would believe it. Nobody has ever seen them before."

"I will coordinate with the Overmind. We can do this if...Do you think the Deucadons would go along with this plan?"

"Absolutely," Rei said. "They told me so."

"Do you know how to contact them?"

"Yeah, kind of. At least I know where to start. I can get MINIMCOM to come and get me and we can try and find them."

"*Then go do it. Go pick them up."*

"Rome, I'll need you to come, too. You're going to have to convince them that they will be safe. They do not trust the Vuduri. Besides, I want you with me just in case things go south when the time comes."

"*All right. I will come with you. You can pick me up shortly, but I want you to wait just a little while longer,"* Rome said in his thoughts.

"Why, sweetheart?" he asked.

"I need to work with the Overmind to choreograph our part. I promise I will let you know when it is time."

"Anything you say, honey. I can't wait to be with you again." His heart leaped in his chest at the thought.

"And I cannot wait to be with you, either, mau emir."

"I've missed you so much, Rome. My heart aches all the time."

"I have missed you too, mau emir. It is as if a part of me is gone. I am no longer whole."

"So...has it been long enough? Can I come get you now?"

Rome laughed gently inside his head. *"Soon, my love, soon."*

"All right, Rome. I'll be ready."

Switching to MINIMCOM, Rei thought to himself, *"Hey MINIMCOM, I need you to be on standby. We need to be ready when the time comes to go get Rome. She's like the Queen of the Vuduri now."*

"At your service, sir," MINIMCOM replied, a bit sarcastically.

"Wise guy!" thought Rei.

"I like that title, Queen of the Vuduri," replied Rome, laughing inside of Rei's thoughts.

Rei just shook his head then laughed to himself. If only the world could see inside his brain. It had to be the craziest place in the entire universe. He tugged at Fridone's shirt, whispered his plan and at the first opportunity, they hopped off of the troop carrier even as it was moving relentlessly toward the Vuduri compound.

"Where are you going?" asked one of the would-be colonists, seeing them jump off.

"I have to go to the bathroom," Rei shouted back to him. He pointed to Fridone. "He's coming with me to watch for 'falling blankets.' We'll catch up in a minute."

Before the man could protest, Rei and Fridone darted into the woods.

Chapter 19

ROME PACED THE ROOM FOR A BIT, ORGANIZING HER THOUGHTS, getting ready for her final conference with the Overmind. Aason could sense her moving about and kicked her to get her attention. While it did not hurt, it was still an odd sensation that never failed to amuse her.

"*Mother, what is happening?*" he asked.

"*I must prepare, my baby. Today is the day I go to see your father,*" she replied.

"When will I get to meet him?"

"*Very soon, my son, very soon. Go back to sleep for now. It will all be over shortly."*

"And then I can come out?" Aason asked.

"*Yes, baby, then you may come out."*

"Oh good. Please hurry. I cannot wait."

"I will go as fast as I can. You rest now."

Rome could feel him settle down again. She went over to her balcony. Since it faced west, Rome could not see Tau Ceti as it made its way up over the eastern ocean. However, from her vantage point, there were some high-flying clouds overhead that reflected its rosy colored light. The sky was brightening. Rome activated her PPT modulation link to the Overmind.

It took the Overmind a little while to get over the shock of the existence of the Deucadons but after it did, it set to work with Rome devising a plan on how it would all go down.

As they were reviewing the plan one last time, Rome said, "*Rei just informed me that the Essessoni will be here shortly."*

"Yes," replied the Overmind, *"my scouts have confirmed this."*

"You must be very careful," Rome thought. "*The sequence of events must be exact. Each move will be followed by a counter-move. You know what the end-game must be."*

"Yes," replied the Overmind.

"I am not talking about just our battle plan. I am talking about all of it. After this is settled, you will not only free the mandasurte, you will free the Vuduri as well. We must stop the asteroid. You will live here and you will thrive."

"You do not need to explain to me," answered the Overmind. *"I understand it all. And I agree. I look back now and I see the disease, the wrong thinking that came here from Earth. To allow the Onsiras to thrive and perpetrate their plan, it is wrong. And immoral. It took you to show this to me. I am getting healthy now. I will do the right thing here. But this awareness, to show me, you are unique."*

"I do not have to be. You have the power to change all of that. Just as I taught Pegus, so too, you must allow him to teach isolation to all of the communicants. You must teach all of them how to turn the connection off and on," thought Rome.

"I will do this. I will follow this course," replied the Overmind. *"However, it reminds me that I have something humorous to tell you."*

"And what is that?"

"When I learned you were coming, I was only concerned with destroying the Essessoni. Your particular fate was irrelevant, of no real concern to me."

"Why is that humorous?" Rome asked.

"Had I known of your powers of persuasion, I would have known to fear you far more than a group of blood-thirsty maniacs from the past."

Rome smiled. *"I am nothing to fear. I only speak the truth."*

"Yes, I know. And that is what the Onsiras fear the most. If the truth ever gets out, all their plans will be lost."

"We must hope."

"Even so, I am glad that you and I got to speak. I am glad that you have helped me see my true position here. I think you saved me and all the Vuduri here. I was sick, as you said, and now I see the path to health. I just think it is amusing that a little girl like you is more powerful than all the armies of old Earth."

Rome laughed out loud. What a wonderful feeling it was, to be able to laugh. She continued. "*As we have discussed, it is the way of the Overmind to see things one way and one way only. Its basic nature is to eliminate dissent by eliminating discussion. An Overmind's final decision, flawed or not, never gets challenged, even in the light of new information."*

"I believe we had what used to be known as tunnel vision," thought the Overmind.

"So now is the time to reach out, to come out of the tunnel. Reach out to the mandasurte, to the Essessoni, to all."

"You know they think I am the enemy," thought the Overmind.

"We will show them you are not. We will show them that you want to learn and that they can be your teachers. They will teach you to love."

"I understand," said the Overmind. *"I want to feel love. In fact, I do feel love. I feel it from you. And for this, I thank you, Rome."*

"You are welcome," Rome thought.

"And to the extent that I understand the concept, I believe I am in love with you."

"That is a very kind thought," Rome said, blushing in her mind. *"But I think we will keep that to ourselves. I can see where that might make Rei jealous."*

"We would not want that to happen, now would we?" said the Overmind acerbically.

"*No*," thought Rome then she straightened herself up. *"Speaking of which, I am going to call him now."*

"I understand," said the Overmind. *"Goodbye and good luck. I hope I survive all of this."*

"You are so maudlin. This is not the end," Rome thought. *"Always remember that. This is just the beginning."*

"Yes, I can see that. Farewell, Rome."

Rome took that as her cue to disconnect the link to the Overmind. She walked to the edge of the balcony, placing her hands on the stone railing there. She shielded her eyes with one hand and scanned the horizon and finally spotted a tiny, shiny, all-black presence, glinting in the early morning sun. She waved to it then closed her eyes to open a channel.

~ ~ ~

Inside the cockpit of the modified tug which was now the starship known as MINIMCOM, Fridone sat in the co-pilot's seat, watching the viewscreens and various instruments. Next to him, in the pilot's seat, Rei sat quietly, just staring out through the cockpit window, watching the sun as it was rising over the Vuduri compound. His reverie was interrupted when his mind was warmed by his beautiful wife's sultry voice who thought to him, "*Rei*?"

"*Yes, sweetheart?*" he replied.

"It is time. Come and get me."

"You bet!" Rei thought enthusiastically.

Then out loud, Rei said, "You heard the woman, MINIMCOM. Go and get her."

"**`Yes, sweetheart,`**" replied the spaceship through a grille mounted on the front panel.

Rei was going to have to have a long talk with that computer someday - just not today.

Chapter 20

ONCE THE ESSESSONI ARMY BROKE THROUGH THE COVER OF THE cane-tree woods, they took up a position along the alluvial plain to the west of the Vuduri compound. The mix of soldiers filed out initially into a wishbone-shaped pattern. From Captain Keller's perspective, they no longer needed the element of surprise. The breadth and power of his weapons would be sufficient. At the front of the line, the particle beam cannons were set within sandbags, giving them a bunker-like appearance. Each cannon was flanked on either side by the troop carriers. Behind them, the ranks stood firm. Each man and woman from the Ark was armed with a laser rifle, flamethrower or a regular automatic weapon.

The battle plan would start with taking out the Vuduri PPT throwers. Keller's scouting reports told him that they were probably the Vuduri's most dangerous weapon. He would try and use the cannons first. They had the longest reach. He had made up his mind that he would use the tactical nuclear warheads only as a last resort.

The rifles, both laser and conventional, were reserved for taking down their aircraft. They would use their laser rifles to kill the pilots and the automatic weapons to destroy the engines. Pretty straightforward stuff.

As far as the Vuduri ground troops, he'd use the cannons to reduce their compound to rubble. That would give them the psychological advantage. If that failed, only then would he bust out the mini-nukes. The strike didn't have to be pretty but it would certainly be decisive.

The flamethrowers would slow down any ground assault. If it came to hand-to-hand combat, each member of the Ark's crew was paired with one of the Ibbrassati, armed with their version of hand weapons, better suited for fighting in close quarters.

Communication was hard, limited to some rudimentary hand-signals. Keller waved to Ionelli who came over to stand beside him, along with Trabunel.

"Get me Bierak," Keller said. "I need to organize the attack. This won't take long but I don't want any of our people hurt by friendly fire." He emphasized his point by waving the assault rifle he was holding.

"He's gone, sir," said Ionelli.

"What?!" Keller sputtered. "Where? When?"

"A few hours ago. He hopped off the troop carrier along with that Fridone guy and disappeared into the woods."

"Damn him!" Keller said. "What a coward. There is something seriously wrong with that boy. Well, I don't have time to go searching for him. We'll discipline him later. Do what you can to get everyone fanned out. I don't want to make it easy on them."

Using a pair of binoculars, Keller could see the Vuduri streaming out of the enclave. Their soldiers were equipped with exotic-looking rifles. Rising up from the airfield to the south were waves of warcraft but rather than coming forward, they hovered over their own troops in a long, wide formation. The Vuduri took up positions from north to south. It was a long line, longer than Keller had anticipated.

Keller's plan was to strike and strike swiftly. The Ibbrassati had haltingly explained to him that there were other Vuduri outposts around Deucado. If the call went out for reinforcements, crossing the ocean would take time, time the Vuduri weren't going to get. Keller figured the Vuduri probably underestimated the capabilities of the older Earth's weaponry anyway. He chuckled to himself, imagining them sitting there in their ivory tower, convinced of their advanced technical prowess. What they did not know was that the Essessoni were not bound by their technological inhibitions and they were going to get hit with things that were unthinkable to them.

"All right, you guys," he said to his troops. "This is it. We hit them fast and we hit them hard. We're taking over this place and nobody is going to stop us." A cheer went up from his men. The Ibbrassati were not sure what he said, but after they saw the reaction of their allies, they cheered as well. After the cheers rippled down, he said, "Get ready for my signal."

Trabunel tugged at his sleeve and pointed up. "Um nefoi," he said. "Um asdrenhi nefoi. Drede-sa ta iudre ciose."

"Huh?" Keller said but he looked up where Trabunel was pointing. Heading straight for the open area between the two warring parties was a sleek, wasp-waisted all-black space ship bristling with PPT generators, plasma thrusters and more.

"Get ready to fire," Keller said desperately.

"Nei sa drede ta um nefoi ta guarre. Drede-sa ta um rapicetir," said Trabunel. "Nei oncantoi eonte." He shook his head and waved his arms to make his point. "Rei," he said finally.

"Rei? You mean Bierak?" Keller asked. Trabunel nodded vigorously.

The ship hovered for a moment then rotated slowly in place. It settled down to land midway between the two forces. The rear cargo door lifted open, a ramp emerged and down it walked Rome and Rei who was holding her elbow to steady her. Fridone, Rome's father, followed behind them. As soon as they were clear, the ramp retracted, the cargo door sealed up and the craft took off straight up, leveling off perhaps 500 feet in the air and hovered there.

After the craft was clear, Rome looked back at the ranks of the Vuduri then forward to the amassed armies of Essessoni and Ibbrassati. She made her way forward with slow but steady progress, Rei at her side. She motioned to Trabunel who came forward. She spoke to him directly.

"E guarre sipra. The war is over," Rome said. Her words were picked up by MINIMCOM from inside of Rei's head and transmitted through the central EG lifter, turning it essentially into a giant PA system. Rome opened up her PPT transducers so that all the Vuduri could hear her thoughts directly.

"Cimi bita e guarre sar axcassi quenti nei cimacer eonte?" Trabunel asked.

"Captain Keller. I Vuduri ceboduleda. The Vuduri capitulate," Rome said. "Cimberdolherei ta dite e dacniligoe cim fica. They will share all technology with you. Fica a um lomoda nei meos lingi ei blenade. You are no longer bound to the planet."

As if on signal, the warcraft and shuttles from the Vuduri side that had been hovering over their troops rotated in place and moved toward the Essessoni backwards. They settled into the space just behind Rei and Rome. After they landed, the pilots and crew exited their craft and began walking back toward the ranks of the Vuduri thus leaving their ships unattended. The choreography was impressive.

"Cimi a osdi bissofal?" Trabunel said. "I qua asde onti sipra equo, Fridone?"

"Monhe volhe fa-lha," Fridone said to him.

"Hold on just one minute," Keller said, moving forward, "This war isn't over until we say it's over."

Ignoring him, Rome said as loudly as she could, "Nei hefare nanhume lude. There will be no fighting. Nis nei vezamis axema ta nei meos papa. We take no more babies." Rome's words were echoed by MINIMCOM's speakers.

Then to Keller, she said, "We will share this planet with you as equals. No more master and slave."

To Trabunel, she said, "Nei meos masdra a ascrefi."

Then, to Keller again, she said, "There is no need for any bloodshed."

"Why should we believe you?" said Keller.

"Because we could defeat you if we wanted to," Rome said firmly.

"How?" Keller asked.

"I will give you a demonstration. Please pull your men back from that cannon." She pointed to the nearest particle beam projector. "I do not want anyone to get hurt."

"Forget it," Keller said.

"Very well," Rome replied. "Have it your way." She snapped her fingers.

Directly above one of the particle beam cannons, a pitch black circle appeared. The air started whistling out of it, like a reverse gale. The black circle began lowering toward the cannon. At the last second, the men manning it scattered. After the circle passed through the space that the cannon occupied, it disappeared. When the circle finally hit the ground, the cannon simply was no more.

"You are getting really good with that trick," Rei thought himself.

"Yes, I am, am I not?" replied MINIMCOM in Rei's head.

"What'd you do to it?" Keller asked.

"It is elsewhere," Rome replied.

Keller narrowed his eyes. “So why capitulate at all?” he asked. “With that weapon alone, you’d have the upper hand.”

“The Vuduri are not stupid,” Rome replied. “I have opened their eyes. The Vuduri now know that the skies belong to the mandasurte, not to the connected. The space lanes belong to the mind-deaf. And to you.”

“What!?” Keller said. “What are you talking about?”

“The Asdrale Cimatiras, the Stareaters, are coming,” Rome said, lifting her eyes upward. “They are drawn to the Overmind, they seek it out and then they render it senseless in order to kill it. There is gravitic leakage from our PPT modulators. The Stareaters are drawn to the Vuduri like moths to a flame.”

She lowered her eyes again to look at Keller. “Never again can Vuduri travel in space without being accompanied by mandasurte,” Rome said fervently. “It is too dangerous. We cannot know where all the Stareaters are. They can appear at any time. The very thing that gives the Vuduri their strength on a planet is their greatest weakness in space.”

Rei spoke up for the first time. “Sir, the Vuduri acknowledge that the first humans on this world deserve to set the rules. If that is your guiding principle, then there is no need for war.”

“Damn straight,” said Keller. “The first of our people on this planet should be allowed to set the rules.”

“You and all your men vow this? That this world belongs to the first Essessoni to set foot here?” asked Rome with a hint of a smile.

“Yes, we vow it,” said Keller. “Everyone should yield to the rightful rulers of this planet. The first people from *my* time to start here.”

“Fica iufou-is. You have heard them,” Rome said to Trabunel and to all the mandasurte assembled there, amplified through MINIMCOM’s projectors and by direct thought to the Vuduri behind her. “Asda munti bardanca eis bromaoris saras humenis ti Essessoni ei ba ti jigi equo. Even Captain Keller acknowledges that this world belongs to the first humans from Garecei Ti Essessoni to set foot here.”

To Rome's left, the air shimmered and two men appeared. They pulled back their hoods and all could see from their build that they were from the older Earth, Rei's Earth.

"Who the hell are they?" Keller asked.

Rei said, "They are the Deucadons. They are descendents of the Ark III, the mission to 82 Eridani. They have been here for 500 years."

Rome interrupted. "According to you, they are the true rulers of this world."

"This is some trick," spat Keller.

"This is naw trick," said Bukky. "My people have been here for half a millennium. We have remained hidden because of the stroids and the flaggin' little people." He jabbed his thumb behind him, at the rows of Vuduri.

"Who are you, really?" Keller asked.

Melloy stepped forward. "This is Bukky, our leader. He is takin' a chance by even showin' himself to ya."

Bukky continued. "I come here to show good faith. We have decided that we will nawt be afraid of the little people any longer. We trust these people, Rei and Rome. We believe them about our common threat. Ya should too."

"This is all bullshit," said Keller. "Just some hocus-pocus to lull us into cooperating so that you can do what you want."

Bukky lifted his arm and pointed his finger directly at Keller. He said in a deep voice, "Captain Keller, I am the lawfully elected governor of this world and yar Commander-in-Chief. Ya report to me. I want ya to stand down."

Keller's jaw dropped. He seemed dazed. Rei stepped in front of his wife and spread his arms to both sides.

"Captain Keller. The Vuduri call us Garecei Ti Essessoni, which means the Killer Generation. Prove them wrong. You need the Vuduri. You need their technology to live in their world. You need the VIRUS units to save the planet. They are offering to lay down their arms. The Deucadons were here first. It is their world. They're willing to live in peace. The Vuduri are willing to live in peace. The Ibbrassati want to live in peace."

Rei turned back to Trabunel who nodded enthusiastically.

Rei continued. “The time has come. You need to take them up on the deal. There is no need to fight each other. They will not take the first shot. Honor your promise to me.”

Rei stepped back and took Rome’s hand. She squeezed and he turned to look at her. She smiled and winked at him and he was shocked to see her rising up into the air. She released his hand and floated forward, toward Keller, until she was, at most, two steps away from him, her eyes the same height as his.

“*MINIMCOM, how did you do that?*” Rei thought to himself.

"Smoke and mirrors, my friend, smoke and mirrors," replied MINIMCOM, pleased with himself.

“*No, come on,*” Rei thought. “*Tell me!*”

"It is just an extended repulsor field. A flying carpet, if you will. If you were standing directly behind her, you would have floated up as well. I think it is a nice effect."

“Sleek,” thought Rei. *“Very sleek.”*

Floating before Captain Keller, all alone there, this tiny woman, eight months pregnant, so vulnerable, made her voice heard loud and clear to the thousands gathered around.

“Captain Keller. You must listen to me. The war is not down here. It is up there.” She pointed straight up. “It is not just control of a planet at stake. It is the very existence of life. There are things coming that are bigger than you and me and the whole world. The time has come to put aside our differences and work as one to protect our world and keep us safe. We are all human. We need to work together if we are going to survive as a species.”

Trabunel put his hand on Keller’s shoulder and said, “Bir qua nei i danda? Nis bitamis sambra mede-lis meos derta," and then he laughed.

“Huh?” Keller said. “What’d he say?”

“He said you can always kill us later,” Rome answered. “Why not give it a chance?”

Keller looked around him. Every one of his crew, all of the Ibbrassati, the Deucadons, all were nodding. Not one of them looked like they wanted a war. It was clear to him that all any of them ever wanted was peace and equality. He lowered his weapon.

“All right, Mrs. Bierak, you win. We’ll give it a try,” he said. All four races shouted in glee, including the Vuduri.

Rei shook his head as he surveyed the whole scene. He hoped some of them would take the time to realize how truly remarkable this was.

Rome floated back to Rei and settled next to him. She let herself relax in a way she hadn't felt in a very long time. The Overmind took the opportunity to address her.

"Good job, Rome," thought the Overmind quietly.

Rome smiled and replied, "*It is just the beginning. My work is over. The rest is up to you.*"

"Then let us start," said the Overmind as the Vuduri moved forward.

Pegus came out to meet them and suggested, in English, that they form a liaison committee to architect how the races would live together. Even as they were doing that, the Vuduri pilots who had abandoned their ships, crossed the lines and each picked an Ibbrassati to "adopt" to begin their training on flying the spacecraft. The very first thing they did was load in the Essessoni equipment and help the Ibbrassati and Essessoni transport it back to their settlement.

Rei held Rome close watching all this occur. After the crowd had dispersed, Rei turned to Rome and said, "You did it, honey. You saved the world this time."

She smiled at him and said, "I guess it was my turn, eh?"

Rei laughed. Just then, Rome doubled over in pain, grabbing her abdomen. Rei kneeled down to hold her hand. He looked up into her beautiful, glowing eyes.

"Sweetheart," he said, "more pain? Is it bad?"

"It is not the same as before," she said. "I think, mau emir, it is time to have our baby." She pointed to the ground.

Rei looked and saw her pant legs were soaked and there was a small puddle pooled around her feet.

"I guess it is," Rei replied.

"Mother," Aason said. *"I am ready."*

"Yes, baby, it is time," Rome thought lovingly.

Even as Rome spoke in her mind, there were three Vuduri running over to her to help her aboard one of the shuttles. The tiny craft lifted into the sky and flew them directly to the courtyard of the Vuduri compound, leaving behind the mix of peoples who were really seeing each other as equals for the very first time.

Chapter 21
(Two days later)

WITHIN THE VUDURI COMPOUND, ROME WAS RESTING WITH HER newborn in her arms. The Vuduri had taken exquisite care in constructing a comfortable room for her to recuperate. Rei was sitting in a chair just watching over the scene. Except for being early, the boy seemed healthy. He cried. He ate. He pooped. He did all the things you'd expect of a baby. That the baby could talk to his mother and father within his mind was still a wonder to Rei. He had gotten used to the concept of mind-to-mind communication in general, but this was a two-day-old baby. Their discussions were always amusing. Aason was capable of adult conversation but the subjects were usually very much that of a newborn. There were times when Aason and Rome used their private PPT-driven channel, which excluded Rei, but that did not bother him. All in all, it was a peaceful respite when compared to the adventure that they had just been through.

The Ibbrassati and the Vuduri were working with MINIMCOM, harnessing his enhanced memron fabricators to build up the supply of starprobes and VIRUS units in preparation for a possible arrival of the Stareaters. The first stage of MINIMCOM's current plan was to create a giant sphere of detection. He was going to send a swarm of starprobes beyond the Oort Cloud in all directions. The early warning system was supposed to give MINIMCOM enough time to react if a Stareater was detected. In theory, MINIMCOM would then transport a group of mandasurte and plant the VIRUS units on an asteroid or comet that was within the path of the Stareater thus following the technique orchestrated by OMCOM back on Dara.

With the T-suppressor, it was possible that some of the Vuduri would go along for the ride but they could not be relied upon to remain conscious if they were to get too close to a Stareater. Sadly, or perhaps fortunately, all Vuduri now knew that the space lanes belonged to the mandasurte, not the Vuduri. Even if the T-suppressors worked, they essentially turned the Vuduri into mandasurte so truly the cosmos belonged to the mind-deaf.

It was so peaceful, so relaxing, that Rei found himself dozing off when Rome awakened him.

"Rei?" she said quietly.

"Yes, sweetheart," he answered her sleepily.

"Our work is not done. We have to go to Earth. And soon."

"Why?" Rei asked. "Do I really want to know?"

"Even though it appears tranquil, the situation is far more dangerous than anyone realizes," Rome replied. "We will never have the life we desire here if we do not act. Word will leak out, somehow and when it does, the Onsiras will send people to undo all that we have accomplished."

"Who are the Onsiras?"

"They are the true enemy. They are hidden behind the Overmind, the samanda within the samanda. The Onsiras are the ones responsible for this prison world. They are the ones who wish to take all the mandasurte from the Earth and put them here. They are controlled by someone or something beyond the reach of the Overmind."

"Why us? Why do we have to go?" Rei asked plaintively.

"The Overmind here explained it to me," Rome replied. "No Vuduri can return to Earth because the Overmind there will connect to them and know immediately what has happened here. The Onsiras will find out and they will send a strike force to kill all the mandasurte."

"So send one of the Ibbrassati," Rei countered.

"No. No mandasurte can go for the very same reason. Once the Onsiras see even one of them returning from Deucado, they will know that something has happened here and unleash the forces of death."

"What about the Deucadons?" Rei asked hopefully.

"No, the only people who can return to Earth with a legitimate excuse are you and me and Aason. The Overmind and I have discussed this and we agree."

Rei sighed. "And here I was enjoying our 20 minutes of peace before the next disaster. I was daydreaming about how nice our life was gonna be here, now that everything was settled."

"It would remain a dream. There can be no peace. Not yet. And there is more. There is yet another fact that you did not know. The most disturbing of all."

"And we have to fix whatever it is, of course. What is it?" Rei asked wearily.

"The Overmind here told me there is an asteroid coming that will strike Deucado in 20 years or so."

"You're kidding me," Rei said. "A big one?"

"Yes," Rome answered sadly, "a planet-killer."

"Figures," Rei scoffed. "Who would be so foolish as to colonize a world that was going to be destroyed?"

"It was not always this way. After all, your people picked this world as your primary target. The Overmind believes it was your spacecraft that jarred the asteroid from its orbit that is now heading for us."

"So that's what hit us?" Rei said. "And now it's headed here? It's like a stupid game of cosmic billiards. Only the Vuduri would pick a doomed planet for a prison world."

"On the contrary," Rome said, "knowing the asteroid was coming in the first place was what guided their selection of this world to imprison the mandasurte."

"Didn't you tell me that people come here thinking it's a new colony? Don't you think somebody, some mandasurte, on Earth would notice something like an asteroid bearing down on this planet?"

"The information has been suppressed. They want it to happen. And according to the Overmind here, the Onsiras have a plan called Silucei Vonel."

"What does that mean, Silucei Vonel?" Rei asked.

"It translates to the 'final solution'," said Rome sadly.

"Final solution? Last time they tried that on Earth, it meant genocide of the Jews during World War II," said Rei worriedly. "Maybe it doesn't mean what you think it means."

"I am afraid it does. That name was not selected by accident. While your history has been suppressed, it has not been completely expunged. Genocide is still genocide."

"So they gather up the mandasurte and bring them here so they can die? Why not just kill them in the first place?" Rei asked as if he were solving a mathematical equation. "It's not like the Vuduri to be so inefficient."

"Not the Vuduri, the Onsiras. It was their hope to keep the asteroid a secret until the event occurred. It would simply appear to be a sad accident and the rest of the Vuduri and the Overmind of Earth would just go on about their business. They would never know it was preordained. Of course, this was before they knew of the Stareaters. Now the Onsiras may decide to accelerate the schedule."

"Has the Overmind here been told of this?"

"No, it was speculating. But that does not change the fact this duty falls upon us," Rome said deadly seriously. "We must stop it. We must stop all of them, somehow."

Rei took a deep breath. "Just once," he said, "I'd like a day off from having to the save the universe." He sighed again. "Of course we'll go, honey. As soon as you're up to it. But can we just take it easy for a little bit longer? To decompress?"

"Yes," Rome said, "another day or so. Then we must go."

"You're the boss…" Rei said, then stopped speaking, noting the sounds of approaching footsteps. Their quiet moment was interrupted by a four-man committee consisting of Captain Keller, Melloy, Rome's father, Fridone, and Pegus. Rei noticed that Captain Keller was limping less even though it had only been three days since he had swallowed one of OMCOM's pills. Rome's father walked over and stroked his daughter's head then patted Aason's very gently.

"Cimi a mau vezar ti nadi?" Fridone asked.

"A muodi pam, Beo. He is fine," Rome answered.

"Yes," said Pegus. "More than that, our genetic analysis tells us that Aason truly is the first of a new breed. He has the traits of the Vuduri, the Essessoni and more. His ability to communicate using gravitic or electromagnetic transmission at will is just the beginning. We cannot even guess at the limits of his capacity."

Keller spoke up. "Bierak, we want to start our mining operations. We want to build a spaceport and a settlement. Do you think we can borrow your little computer ship to help us?"

"I'll ask him," Rei answered. "But there's something that Rome and I have to do first. After that, I'm sure it won't be a problem."

Just then, Trabunel came rushing into the room along with one of the Ibbrassati. The man's forehead was bleeding.

"What happened?" Rome asked.

"Dhaitira," said Fridone to the man. "I qua a ub?"

"Ume mulhar gilbaiu ta bolidi a pedau-ma bere vire. Saquasdriu i nefoi," replied the mandasurte.

"What did he say?" asked Keller.

Rei translated, his tone was incredulous. "He said a woman came onboard, and knocked him and the pilot out. He said she hijacked one of the spaceships," He closed his eyes. "*MINIMCOM*," he spoke inside his head. *"Are you nearby? Do you see a spaceship leaving Deucado?"*

"I am nearby and yes, I see a ship leaving. Here..." A humming sound issued from the general vicinity of a low table near the window. Above the table, the air shimmered and sparkled. Out of nowhere, there was a whoosh and a popping noise. A small, black conical object appeared, settling on the surface of the table.

"What is that thing?" Rei asked out loud.

"A image projector," MINIMCOM replied from a speaker built into the object. **"I will relay what the starprobes are seeing."** A portal opened on one side and a beam of light shot out illuminating the far wall with a dark background punctuated by bright points of light, a star field. The field of vision panned until it focused on a Vuduri craft, traveling backwards with its plasma thrusters slowing it down.

Pegus stared at the screen. His eyes defocused. He shook his head and became alert again. "It is Sussen," he said sadly.

"MINIMCOM, can you stop her?" Rei asked but even as he was speaking, the ship turned and entered the dark black circle. Just like that, it was gone.

"Rei, it is happening." Rome said sharply. "We cannot allow her to get to Earth first. We must go. Now!"

A Preview of *Redemption*
(The Rome's Revolution Saga: Book 3)

Location: Earth

A BLINDING LIGHT APPEARED IN THE SKY AS THE CRAFT ACTIVATED its floodlights, illuminating Rei and Rome and a broad circle of sand. Instinctively, Rei pushed Rome behind him as the peculiarly shaped vehicle flew overhead then settled into the sand just in front of them. The craft was a long tube on stilts, like a bizarre form of a bus or helicopter fuselage. It was almost insect-like. It was rounded with rows of windows along the sides and four oversized EG lifters, one at each corner mounted at the end of the stilts. Rei realized that it was very similar to the craft that had transported him from the Vuduri palace on Deucado.

Rei put his hand up to block the light from shining directly into his eyes. He saw that a door in the side lowered and there were stairs built into the back of the door. Very quickly, six armed men, dressed completely in black, ran down the steps and came right at them.

"Rome?" Rei asked, not sure how to finish the question.

The strange men circled around Rome and Rei until they formed a complete ring.

"What is this?" Rome called out loudly. "We have done nothing wrong."

Wordlessly, one of the men poked at Rei with the barrel of a weapon while another waved at the transport. It was not hard to figure out their intentions.

"Don't you guys have to have a warrant or something," Rei said in English. The nearest soldier bent forward and looked Rei in the eye. The soldier's eyes were dark black. In the reflected glow the craft's harsh floodlights, Rei could see they were cloudy and flat. They had no life to them. They reminded Rei of a shark's eyes.

"Come with us," the solder said hoarsely, in English. The men behind them pushed them forward.

"What do we do, Rome?" Rei asked, resisting the pressure.

"There are more of them than us," Rome said. "And they are armed. I think we must go with them."

She moved around in front of Rei and started walking toward the craft.

"What about A..." Rei called after her but stopped himself.

"Come," Rome said and she started up the steps built into the ramp. Rei paused at the base of the stairs. "*MINIMCOM,*" he called out, using the cellphone in his head. "*Can you hear me?*"

"Yes," replied the starship. **"Why are you contacting me?"**

"*I think we're in trouble.*"

"What happened?"

"*We just got arrested by a bunch of armed guards with dead eyes.*"

"That does not sound encouraging," MINIMCOM replied.

One of the troops pushed Rei in the back. Rei started walking up the stairs as slowly as he could. "*Where are you?*" he asked, stopping at the top.

"I am roughly 4000 kilometers due north of your previous position. The Aleutian Islands are directly ahead of me."

"*I think you'd better come back,*" Rei said. "*And pronto. Nothing good is going to come of this.*"

"On my way," MINIMCOM replied. **"I will be there as quickly as I can."**

"*Thanks, buddy,*" Rei thought as he bent his head down and stepped in the cabin.

"No problem, erp, <click>," said MINIMCOM and the connection was cut.

Rei's eyes widened. He tapped his temple as if to clear the receiver but nothing changed. The transport was somehow shielded against the apparatus in his head. The cabin was filled with a dozen rows of spartan-looking seats and not much else. The soldiers placed Rei on one side and Rome on the other.

One soldier sat between Rei and the aisle. Another did the same for Rome. The other four soldiers sat in the seats in front of them and behind them.

Rei looked out the window and even though there was no sensation of motion, he could see the ground dropping below.

"Where are you taking us?" Rei asked but the soldier ignored him.

The craft rotated in place and headed across the southern part of Maui, rising as it went. Rei could see the gigantic crater of Haleakala to the north. In a short while, they were over the ocean. It was not long before they came upon the Big Island of Hawaii. They cut across the interior skirting around the peak of Mauna Loa, then headed due east.

Rei looked over at Rome but he could not see her because of the guard sitting between them. Rei turned and looked out the window again. In the pale moonlight, Rei could see patterns that he guessed were vegetation interspersed among black, volcanic rock. As the pilot brought the craft around, the caldera of Kilauea rose up in front of them and they climbed again, following its rise to its peak. The transport stopped its horizontal motion and rotated in place, hovering over the huge crater. The mouth of the crater was over half a mile across, dwarfing the small craft. The pilot lowered them straight down, coming to rest just above the floor of the dormant volcano.

Activating the floodlights again, the transport inched its way forward into a tunnel built into the side. After a short time, a slight jostle indicated they had landed. The soldiers arose and formed a phalanx, escorting Rei and Rome down the boarding stairs.

Once they were on the ground, the soldiers grasped them on their arms and the remaining soldiers moved behind them, holding out their rifles. Prodding them along, they walked forward and entered a slightly smaller tunnel. The roof was high, perhaps 30 feet over their heads. As Rei looked around he decided this was a fairly old lava tube. The walls were real, not Vuduri glop. Along the walls were dimly lit globes separated by great distances, but there were enough of them to see their way walking along the hard ground.

As they walked along the tunnel, Rei could see they were in an elaborate underground complex. Occasionally, there were doorways cut out of the living rock but it wasn't until they were taken to the apparent end of the hallway that they stopped. One of the soldiers opened a door and motioned that they were to go through. As they entered the room, it was only slightly easier to see. There were aerogel panels covering up some of the rock not quite reaching the ceiling. However, the panels did emit the usual diffuse light that seemed to emanate from all Vuduri-made materials. The ceiling was partially tiled but above it, Rei could see lava rock, dark gray and porous.

Rei was marched to an aerogel bench along the right wall. One of the soldiers took a large metal loop and placed it over Rei's chest and arms and clamped him in place. A second soldier put another ring of metal around Rei's ankles.

While this was taking place, Rome was moved to the opposite side of the room, to an examining table that reminded Rei of the one used back on Deucado when Pegus set about reconnecting Rome to the Overmind. The soldiers lifted Rome up and placed her on the table.

"What are you going to do to her?" Rei exclaimed. The soldiers ignored him.

Four of the soldiers, including the two armed with rifles, left the room, leaving only two remaining who took up positions by the door. They each had a holster holding a strange sort of hand weapon. The weapons looked somewhat like pistols but their barrels had a flared end instead of a straight tube.

"What do you think they want?" Rei called out to Rome. "The Vuduri already sentenced you. Why does there have to be more?"

"I do not know," Rome answered. "You saw their eyes."

"Yeah," Rei replied sadly. He decided to try and contact MINIMCOM again.

"Hey buddy," he called out in his mind.

"Yzz, brr, bipp. Yzz, brr, bipp," was the reply. The pulsating, buzzing noise was so annoying that Rei had to turn the circuit off. He tried connecting to Rome directly but failed. The only thing he heard was more static. He looked at Rome's face and based upon her expression, she must have tried the same thing and failed as well.

Rei surveyed the room. Several racks filled with electronic equipment were bolted to the wall to the left of where Rome was sitting. He noted one chassis with a blinking block of lights that seemed synchronized to the buzzing in his head. He looked to his right, at the far wall on the opposite side of the room from the door and saw tht it was completely blank, albeit a little grimy. Based upon the layout of the room, it was entirely likely that the lava tube continued beyond the wall but there was no way to tell for sure.

About ten minutes later, one of the soldiers reached over and opened the door. In came three people. Two of them were wearing the Vuduri equivalent of white lab coats which were in stark contrast to the black uniforms worn by the guards. The third person was a petite blonde woman wearing a standard issue Vuduri white jumpsuit. Rei recognized her immediately and his heart sank.

The woman walked over to where Rome was sitting.

"Hello, Estar," Rome said in Vuduri, somewhat dispassionately.

"Hello, Rome," replied the woman with contempt in her voice.

"What do you want with us?" Rei called out to her.

Estar leaned in, staring into Rome's eyes and said, "We require some answers."

"What kind of answers?" Rome asked.

"The truthful kind," Estar replied.

Made in the USA
San Bernardino, CA
09 January 2020

62906992R00117